I0548199

A NOTE ON THE AUTHOR

Patrick Stephen Clinen lives in New South Wales, Australia. The Will of the Wisp is his second novel.

The Will of the Wisp

or

The Friar's Lantern

P.S.Clinen

The Will of the Wisp

First Published In 2017 By

P.S. Clinen

Copyright © 2014 P.S.Clinen

All rights reserved.

ISBN: 0-646-97232-4
ISBN-13: 978-0-646-97232-9
More by the author can be found at

www.psclinen.com

For Constance Mackness.

"The years between our lives would blight our paths to ever link. But from our family tree, we'll write with writer's painterly ink."

Also by P.S.Clinen:

Tenebrae Manor

A Boy Named Art

CONTENTS

ACKNOWLEDGMENTS

Special thanks to my sister Elizabeth for editing. As always, thank you to my wife Edie for her encouragement and support. More than ever this work is dedicated to my family, of which their importance only became more apparent in the years I spent working on this book.

Prologue - Ignis Fatuus
Savonia, Finland 1863

"Like cliffs which had been rent asunder; A dreary sea now flows between, But neither heat, nor frost, nor thunder, Shall wholly do away, I ween, The marks of that which once hath been."

- Samuel Taylor Coleridge

There was every indication of a storm brewing. The autumn, when the year is closest to death while still remaining alive – would be snuffed out by the coming storm. Vaporous vipers of mist coiled about the trees, adorning the cobwebbed forest. They hung from the branches; slithered over root and rotted leaves, gliding silently down the hillside until they slid over the surface of the slowly freezing lake, coating the land with death, clouding over the decay of plant matter that sighed upon the cold earth in soggy clumps. The emaciated branches clung desperately to the last of the leaves, although those star-shaped growths were long dead and shrivelled at the caress of late November wind; they would offer no further comfort. The lake ruffled under the skimming fingers of wind, and above, reflected and multiplied by the mirrored surface, thousands of small lights flickered like candles. They danced of their own accord, phantasmic and mysterious, though none could claim ownership of them. They were not fireflies. They were not the eyes of a myriad of beasts. Nor were they the oil lanterns of travellers on this ill-frequented forest path. The will-of-the-wisp - *ignis fatuus* - hovered like eldritch comets against the evening backdrop of the lake.

Accentuating the natural din of the forest, a certain foreign sound danced across the staff lines of the gale in pianissimo patters. Through the meditative rush of wind it was betrayed not by its volume, but rather the intrusiveness of such noise. A noise that did not belong in this wild scene - it was the roar of peoples. It was the thunderous clap of hooves. A fallen tree, hollowed out so that its rotted shell could offer sanctuary, housed the fearful huddle of a couple in hiding. They clung to one another, cursing the sharp breaths that escaped their lips in audible utterances - a concomitant of both cold and fright. The man cradled the woman as though she were a wounded bird, albeit his strong arms offered little warmth or protection from the elements, as such the both were wracked with shivers. He glanced at her dark head; wisps of black hair strung themselves over the florid beauty of her face, which presently upturned to his. Her eyes, of a piercingly beautiful green, betrayed the assailing fear that mounted in her breast. The look she gave belied the falsity of his confidence; a look that desperately implored that they had not pressed far enough into the forest to escape their predator. The man knew this to be true, and the fear of his mistress only further aggravated his composure. There was little he could do but accept that they were trapped.

He stifled a cough as the woman buried her head in the billows of his cloak. She looked up again, imploring, "The wind is wild! The trees are alive! Surely none would see us moving through the forest!"

Her urgent whisper hissed through the wind so that it was lost as soon as it was uttered; the man's heart lurched nonetheless, and he begged her silence. He did not respond immediately, but instead gazed out carefully from behind the tree to where the sky reddened above the canopy. He opened his mouth to speak, but the words choked in his throat and he cursed the audible baritone of his own murmurings, "The sun will soon set. It is then that we can make a move."

The woman said nothing, but the tear that streaked down her face was enough to shatter the man's heart and dash any intrepidness from his composure.

A skewbald stallion strode betwixt the birch boles. The pelt of the horse shone with an alpine white, splotched in various places with an autumnal auburn, giving it the very embodiment of the early winter forest through which it trotted. Its rider sat hunched and hollow, a ghostly husk atop saddle, drained of his mental energy. His eyes glazed with an unspeakable rage, a rage that increased with each passing second. He strained his ears, but the wind quite obviously impeded whatever it was he was listening for, and his face contorted to a grimacing snarl. Behind him, a small cavalry of horsemen followed obediently, faceless and sombre, as though they were mere trailing shadows of the first rider shifting with the fading light.

"We've but little time sir," one of them murmured, "The night will shield them."

"Don't you think I know that?" snapped the skewbald rider.

He wheeled his horse around with difficulty, the uneven forest floor proving troublesome. From beneath his wild, greying hair his gaze cut deep into his henchmen. It was a glare that they feared, a glare that spoke more than words ever could. Yet still he barked, "Find her. I do not care what it takes. I will have her returned!"

"Sir," came a cry, "what of the man?"

Here the skewbald rider flew into a rage, withdrawing his sword and aiming its blade skyward, "I care not what becomes of that devil! Let him die by your sword or by the unforgiving forest! Just return *her* to me!"

The men dispersed, taking unique paths through the trees, while the skewbald rider steadied his stallion and again cursed through his teeth.

The woman sobbed wretchedly from the shelter of the fallen tree. She watched as the man crept out from their hiding spot and surveyed the surroundings. He turned back to her with a new vigour in his determination.

"We need to make for the lake. If we can get there unseen, their horses will not be able to travel down the steep embankment."

"Could he have assumed us to have made further ground?"

"That is what I am hoping. Come."

Fighting against the trembling in her legs, she arose and followed him into the trees.

Having lost sight of his men, the skewbald rider continued down the sodden path. The forest oozed with damp; the freezing moisture dripping from the trees like cold sweat, while the ground beneath his horse's hooves shifted as they struggled on.

She surely cannot have gotten far in these conditions, not without a horse or provisions.

He cursed the wind as it cut coldly into him. About his body drifted a vibrant vigour; truly the forest was alive. Through the trees, he could see the sludge-like surface of the lake some distance down the hill, and cursed the ghost lights that appeared in the corners of his vision. Those mischievous fairies of luminance gave the impression of the torches of wandering travellers; he vehemently hoped one of them would illuminate his renegade wife. But each floating mote of light that met his gaze brought nothing with it, only adding fuel to his fury.

Curse those lights!

He would then shoot to attention, for from a distance came an otherworldly holler. A shiver rattled down his spine, and it would take the skewbald rider a few seconds to comprehend the cry was not that of some eldritch beast, but rather a twofold bellow of man and horse. Had his wife been found? The stallion was kicked briskly into a gallop, its hoof claps underlining its nervous braying, for the trees were close and the ground uneven. More voices began to permeate in the forest, and for a moment the rider would again feel a mysterious uneasiness. Something sinister seemed to lurk in the trees, an unseen charlatan of mischief that had the rider's blood going cold. But no, it could not be a phantom - those voices indeed belonged to his men, confirmed to him as he entered a small clearing where the cavalry was huddled around a thrashing mass of cloth and flesh. Dismounting, he brandished his whip and moved towards them.

"Stand aside!" he barked, "At last…"

But he would not see that which he desired. Below the party of horsemen lay a crippled mare that complained in a sickening whinny, its rider pinned painfully beneath its girth.

So this is what made that awful moan.

"A rabbit warren, sir," said one of the men, "she caught her foot in it."

"You mean you have not found *her* yet?"

"N-no sir. Nowhere to be seen, and we must turn back to the house! This pair needs attention and the sun is all but gone!"

"I'll have you all freeze to death before we turn back. We are not turning back until my wife is recovered!"

"Sir," cried another man, "I beg you to reconsider. We -"

"Get the man out from beneath that animal."

The fallen rider, a young boy only recently of age, limped gingerly on his leg, bracing himself against his comrades while the mare continued to groan on the ground. Before the men could react, the skewbald rider snatched his blunderbuss and shot the beast, instantly silencing it.

"Sir!"

The astonished riders gaped, instantly taken aback.

The clumsy weapon had been enough to snuff out the life of the injured horse, the eyes of the men dropping as their leader glared at each of them one by one.

"Find her."

From the edge of the clearing the crows scattered; black wing beats pounded the air, and through the tousle of midnight feathers the skewbald rider saw what he was looking for. Those eyes, those incomparable green eyes stared fixedly upon him; fear rooting the woman to the spot. In a second both were running. The rider trailed his renegade wife with cumbersome steps, the heavy blunderbuss his burden. Amongst the branches that brushed against his face as he ran he could discern another figure - his old friend, his betrayer.

So it is as I feared.

He pursued the couple desperately, the treble struggling with the elements that pressed on them at all sides. The wind roared, the branches whipped and struck, the mud shifted beneath their hurried flight. They rumbled down the hill with reckless abandon, the trio locked in a futile stalemate where neither party was advancing upon or moving further towards escape.

"Harlot!" roared the pursuer, "Cease this amour! You would forsake me? You would forsake your children?!"

Bursting onto the lakeside, the renegade man tripped and slid painfully across the thick ice that coated the surface. His attacker wasted no time in leaping upon him, at last realising the uselessness of his lumbering blunderbuss and withdrawing instead a small dagger from his belt. The two men fought on the ice, hurling their fists in a flurry of primal fury. The ice groaned as both men were slammed into the frozen surface in the struggle. Yet despite his blind focus upon his abhorred rival, neither man would be deaf to the tiny cry that escaped the blue lips of the woman they fought for. Still clasping at each other's collars, they turned to where she had slid further from the shore onto the ice shelf. Both had not realised the extent of their brawl sending an ominous fissure between her and the safety of the shore, and now all that accompanied the wind's howl was the blood-curdling crack of splitting ice. For a second that seemingly lasted for an eternity the treble was frozen in fear, the woman's eyes bulging with awful terror, before at last the horrible groan of the ice grew louder and she was plunged into the inky lake water. Her scream would only sound for a moment before it was smothered by the frigid needles of the tarn, while her husband and lover could only watch in horror as the prize of their jealously was lost beneath the darkness of the lake. Above the wind came the very same moan heard earlier by her husband, though perhaps it was merely the trickery of the foreboding nature surrounding. For when both men were able to wrest their eyes from that wretched spot - that black pool that intruded upon flawless ice - they could observe the ignis fatuus, the eyes of the will-o-the-wisp staring down upon their treachery.

I : The Journal of Pinnacle Tricks
Somewhere between Moscow and Saint Petersburg, 1888
"By a route obscure and lonely, haunted by ill angels only…"

- Edgar Allan Poe

I have always felt somewhat of an outsider. This being not so much a revelation at present - rattling away on a Petersburg bound train - but rather the situation pending has brought the idea to the forefront of my mind. Seems that all I do is irrelevant - perhaps pleasing to some other, some higher person(s), done merely due to the 'checkbox' style of life I lead. It is true that I have had many friends; true I have had many an adventure, many a ruse that would define me as unique in my own mortal shell. Furthermore, I've a lovely wife, comfortable living and a lowly position in a respectable industry. And yet still I find myself wrecked with a most unshakable melancholy. Would that I could wrest the beast from my shoulders, but at times I would surmise that the Good Lord intends a few unlucky (?) souls to carry the world's sadness. I am one of those souls. Yet at times I conclude that I am merely overthinking things; placing myself - just another young man - in loftier echelon than my peers. Perhaps it is the torture of an artist; that distinct and ever-present lack of satisfaction. The curse of intellect (Pah! How boorishly arrogant I sound) that has plagued great minds in the past. Ignorance must truly be bliss as they say, yet what purpose would life hold if the pursuit of artistic completion were non-existent? Would I howl and throw myself into the North Sea shoals, or would I be too ignorant (read: happy) to resort to such drastic measures?

The vendor just came past. Observing his wares - an

assortment of sandwiches and coffee - I saw our roles
reversed. What if I were to throw aside the 'ideal career'
for the life of a vagabond? I could roll up and down the
Siberian rail tracks and exchange goods for those little
Russian coins. Or I could be a porter, two limbs dangling
from the side of this roaring locomotive, feeling naught
but the polar winds racing upon me, and one of those
wonderful Russian hats atop my head (I believe they call it
a ushanka). But I say all this fleetingly. What I want is to
feel like my part in this great play of *life* is of substance.
Right now, instead of basking in the centre stage spotlight
of my own existence, I am but a nameless extra lurking
against the backdrop. Is this not *my* life? Who is
responsible for the change I desire - is it myself? I am too
flustered to write further.

A nap did me well. How uncouth I sound in my
previous ramblings! Thank goodness for the journal - the
only place where my stature can slip discreetly. Though I
fear now my sleep will be inhibited this evening, for the
sun is setting yet I feel as spritely as if it were morn. It
seems the sun remains somewhat low in the sky anyway,
such must be the case in this near-Arctic latitude. Though
further dropped towards the horizon and to that extent
seemingly closer to me, the sun does little to warm the
bones. But I must say it accentuates the Siberian beauty
outside the train window. How the view has changed since
Moscow! We must be nearing the coast, for the high
farmlands and snow-coated crags have given way to low
lying taiga and lakes. Lakes, one would say - were they not
completely hidden beneath ice. Only the flatness of terrain
betrays the water that hibernates beneath. It is a most
exquisite twilight scene; would that I could capture it and
sketch its likeness justly! But my pencils are stowed deep in
my portmanteau, so I may only *describe* it here. I have
gathered from my readings that the birch tree is the
national emblem of this vast land, and having heard only
stories of the immensity of Rus[1], I must say that to

observe it in person becomes quite humbling. I am but a speck on the vast Eurasian continent and perhaps those etched white birch boles are but prison bars withholding knowledge that I am never to know – knowledge of what lies beyond that furthest tree, that expanse of frozen lake. Oh, to travel in Russia! I am indeed a fortunate man; I would do well not to complain of ennui.

The porter spoke little English (a barrier proving rather cumbersome in this Slavic land), yet a fellow gentleman passenger informed me that we would soon alight at Petersburg. I remain somewhat wary to be so far East of London, but such has been my vocational calling - Mr. Fairlie was far from gentle in his jettisoning me off on this mission. Apparently, I must reclaim a few items left to him in the will of a recently passed friend. I must say though - he did not seem to care much for my condolences; such seems to be his way. Still, it would be nice to receive some recognition for my loyalty. Such accolades come infrequently to the simple servant.

---

[1] *Rus:* Archaic title for the land and peoples of modern Russia.

II : Rozalina

Saint Petersburg, Russia, 1888

"Everywhere across whatever sorrows of which our life is woven, some radiant joy will gaily flash past."

-      Nikolai Vasilievich Gogol

The lanterns that lined the street pulsed like a divine oracle. They linked together as a chain cutting through the darkness, casting their luminance defiantly so that the snow beneath was bestowed a hostile orange glow, a glow that flickered to a certain radius before weakening into blue, and finally black. That was until the next lantern came sweetly into view, a vessel of salvation, a pathway to Valhalla. The Nevsky Prospekt – that gallant thoroughfare splitting Saint Petersburg entwine and plunging its crooked end into the Neva River – where Anichkov's horses[2] march proudly. Those four riders - Earth; that voluptuous matron, of balanced warmth and power, that of beauty defined in the cold ground of Neva's banks. The roads hardened with the sleet of hundredfold winters. Air; that angel child that flutters down from the North on chilling streams, but she is a charlatan. Little demon of frigid fangs, she bites. She steals the heat of life with her knives. Water; who carves his paths through this Siberian land, fills the craters with torrents from above, who feeds the Neva and all her brethren with Baltic breath. And Fire; that most

---

[2] *Anchikov's horses:* The Anchikov Bridge (1841–42); famous construction on the Nevsky Prospekt, bridging the Fontanka River. The bridge itself is adorned with four 'Horse Tamers' – marble sculptures designed by Russian sculptor Pyotr Karlovich Klodt.

haughty of elements; rash of foot, perilously toeing the equilibrium of its potency. Whereby one may have their very soul snuffed into ash by his flame, the chilled vagabond can hide behind his valiant shield and stave off the freezing death. Those four elements that combined to form the fabric of Saint Petersburg; the Nevsky Prospekt running through its centre like a spine - maybe that of a leaf - where the streets twisted their mangled forms from this spine like veins; veins that throbbed with the vibrant life of Russia - pride, joy, heartiness in an otherwise bleak land.

Across the crisp roads there came a flutter. Weaving betwixt the alleys overseen by the oil lanterns it flurried, threading the winter scene with intrusive stitch - the slip of a paintbrush on what would otherwise be a masterpiece. Stitched as it was with muted colour it scattered icy pebbles of snow powder with boots that crunched in sombre echoes. A phantom not unlike a beating of a butterfly wings as Nevsky Prospekt slumbered. It seemed foreign in the witching hour silence and the speed in which the shadow ran portrayed an intruder who knew they must escape. On a sudden the shadow stopped and from a dingy shawl two globular eyes stared inquisitively. Yet it was not the eyes that piqued with purpose – rather the side effect of ears straining to hear. Halted beneath a lantern the shadow revealed itself to be a young woman; a young woman who, upon realising that she had in fact not heard a thing, resumed her mad dash back to the warmth of the lodge. She is Rozalina, and though it would appear that no-one hurried her on her way at this hour, she knew that it would only be a matter of time before the bells of Peter and Paul chimed thrice, and she would find herself robbed of the hot tea and bread given only to prompt servants. The alleys slid from the Nevsky Prospekt like capillaries, and just before the great arch that led to the Winter Palace[3]

---

[3] *Winter Palace:* Lavish residence of Russian monarchs up

Rozalina swung down a lane alongside a frozen canal. A few carriages lay dormant on the sidewalk gathering snow, while one or two unfortunate doormen stood vigil with frost settling on their ushankas. Roza paid them no mind and soon disappeared down a stony flight of steps that led to the back door of Ignis Errand Inn[4]. The door slammed, and above her apple-cheeked face the lantern swung with the incoming gust. She breathed heavily, face prickled with sweat that had instantly frozen. Her body was coated in a tepid damp, protesting to dashing through subzero Saint Petersburg at 3am. But it had not been in vain. The cook Sergei had not yet thrown yesterday's loaves to the felines. In realising that her ghastly shift had only just begun Rozalina sighed and removed the shawl from her still cold head, revealing a tight bun of red-blonde hair. It was a good haul this morning; the inn being somewhat slow in business during the winter months meant that Sergei often over-compensated and baked too much bread for customers that did not exist. At this rate, she would be able to take some home to the flat. Anything was better than her elderly mother's skilly. She stuffed some loaves into her bag and kept one to eat now. If she hurried she could brew and drink her tea before Maria caught her slacking. The spiral stairs creaked beneath her footsteps as she ascended towards the lobby. She peered into the reception - why she attempted to be stealthy at this point was anybody's guess; the stairs were already terribly noisy - and saw the chair was vacant. Maria must have already left. Rozalina felt her heart accelerate; how long had the inn been untended? Perhaps Maria had just left. She could

---

until the Russian Revolution in 1917.

[4] *Ignis Errand Inn:* Ignis deriving from Latin meaning 'fire'. Ignis Fatuus (foolish fire) – another name for the will-of-the-wisp. In this case 'ignis' might insight the word 'ignorant', reflecting the 'ignorant errand' that Pinnacle Tricks is subject to.

always pin the blame on the weather for being late to work. A half-truth to be sure, but who, in all honesty is prompt to a 3am start? In her own opinion, Roza was already early.

The fire had dwindled to mere embers, the cold from outside already starting to seep under the door. Roza stoked at the ashes and rekindled the flames, before brewing her pot of cheap tea over it. While the water boiled, she paced about the room shivering. From the kitchens, she could discern the sound of flour bags slumped onto the floor, the clang of pans and rolling pins - Sergei was clearly only beginning his shift as well. The auburn warmth of Ignis Errand Inn soon returned with the strengthened fireplace, and Rozalina was at last able to relax her narrow shoulders and cease shivering. The broom stood propped against an ornamental bookshelf, a pile of soot and dust clumped on the floor near it. Maria must have grown fed up and left. For one who kept such a strict reign on her employees, she had little discipline herself. Roza sat at the desk with her tea and examined the books. Only one name was scribbled on its pages - Maria's handwriting. It was a name she could not even try to pronounce; undoubtedly it was a foreigner, supposedly he had arrived yesterday evening. Roza looked up at the ceiling and tried to imagine the mysterious guest on the floor above sleeping in one of the ill-made beds the inn offered.

"Mercy on the fool." she muttered to herself.

The walls muttered discreetly; wind rattled the panes, and just as Roza had begun to lose herself in the hypnagogic trance of her own reflection in those panes, another face appeared before her suddenly. Her heart lurched as a gaunt face shielded by emaciated hands peered about the room from the other side of the glass. In a moment, she recollected herself and swore at her own foolishness - it was but a man on the street looking into the inn. Deciding he seemed harmless enough, Roza grasped a tangle of keys in her slight hands and procured one towards the front door lock. The door blew forward of its own accord, propelled by a howling wind, and racing along this slipstream the thin man also made ingress. He was of slender build, a bird's nest of hair dishevelled by winter gales topping his snow-struck head. Normally one of perfunctory boldness, Rozalina could not help but feel intimidated when the man began chattering a foreign language to her. He paced the room shivering, oblivious to the snow and dirt that traced behind him in clotted expulsions. And when he realised that he was indeed messing up the place he panicked and stuttered some more, clicking his fingers and scratching at his head in frustration.

Between his incoherent ramblings, she could discern a treble of similar phonics almost recognisable; "Ahn-glee-skee?"

The man's teeth chattered; "Uh, uh, ahn-glee-skee?"

Roza shook her head apathetically; "Nyet."

English! So it must be English that this man spewed! She smirked - he was exactly how she'd imagined an Englishman; impuissant with a curious whimsy. But where was Maria? Rozalina did not know a word of English and surely this man was the mysterious guest they had been expecting.

"Only Russian," she replied in her native tongue.

The silence that followed between the two cut sharper than the knives of wind out in the street. The brow of the strange man furrowed; his teeth gritted and he brought onto his face a look of helpless frustration. He sighed vexingly and Roza struggled to clear her mind and figure out what to do with him. She would not need to make any such decision, at that moment a stocky woman raced into the inn at similar speed to the Englishman before her. She is of course, Maria - the owner of Ignis Inn.

Relieving herself of her hooded tan coat she convulsed with a shiver and shuddered audibly. Between the strange man and Roza the tension shattered at the entrance of a third party; yet it would be short lived as Maria launched into a passionate tirade.

"Good Lord! Like herding a sheep you are! Making this old woman rush about in the December snows! The very idea!"

Roza took a moment to realise that Maria was addressing the strange man; she wondered whether she should inform her superior that the man was English, but she was always hesitant to correct her. What followed was a confusing exchange to the younger pair in the room, for Maria was somewhat bilingual and at last there was a bridge between the English and Russian of the man and woman. But she switched between the two tongues with such swiftness that it became taxing to follow.

Addressing the man, "You don't show, I finish my shift, I see you - the only man out at this hour looking so unbelievably lost! I call to you and you run! But in the end you run to the very place you are meant to be!"

"You are the proprietress?" the man asked, "Here I was thinking I was to be harassed by some Russian gypsy! A thousand pardons!"

"Ignorant English," Maria muttered, "You sought Ignis Errand Inn? You are here then."

The man's spirits visibly lifted and he threw his hands into the air, "This is the inn? Praise! At last I find it. I became hopelessly lost when I alighted at Moscow Station; and seeing as though I do not speak your fine language, I could not find any driver who might assist."

"Nevsky Prospekt is a very long street." said Maria, "She is the pride of our most excellent Saint Petersburg."

The man threw out his hand, "Pinnacle Tricks. I am very pleased to -"

Maria instantly turned to Rozalina and shot in Russian, "Roza, you skinny fool! Grab the man some blankets!"

And turning back to Tricks in English, "You are most welcome to our Mother Russia."

Rozalina fumbled through a nearby closet as Maria stamped her foot, "Faster, villain! I'll clip the ears off your very head!"

And again to Tricks, "We hope you will be comfortable; Petersburg is most chilly this time of year."

Allowing Roza to take his coat Tricks could only agree, "You do not need to remind me! I had thought I could not be colder on that trip to the highlands of Scotland as a boy but... Well, as you just said."

"Goodness, child! Not those blankets; they are the dirty laundry!" and to Tricks, "How was your journey from Moscow?"

Tricks moved to offer help to the ladies but was waved away by an increasingly cranky Rozalina.

"Uh, most agreeable madam." said Tricks, "But I have been travelling all week long and am very much eager to rest."

The Russian ladies seemed to tire of the foreigner's small talk; Rozalina loaded herself up with Tricks' belongings and followed her superior up the narrow stairwell. She kept her head down and eyes traced on the steps, lest Maria would turn about and reprimand her further. Pinnacle Tricks meanwhile tried desperately to display some of the chivalry he was wont to exhibit, but Roza was in utmost refusal to allow him to help with the bags. The steps were steep; Tricks wondered how they would hold the weight of three people as well as the luggage he had hauled all the way from England. The summit of the stairs ended in a sharp left turn that led to a narrow hallway. Above them the lamps glowed with a dim light that added an overall eeriness to the Inn. Pinnacle shuddered at the eldritch thoughts that crept into his mind - here he was in a foreign country, in a strange hotel. He could not help but think of those gothic tales of Walpole[5]

---

[5] *Walpole:* Horace Walpole (1717–1797) British writer. His novel *The Castle Of Otranto* (1764) is often cited as the first

and Radcliffe[6]. Were Rozalina the apparition of some long dead maiden his nightmarish imagination would be complete. Invariably he would remain shaken, for Maria veered suddenly to the side and disappeared into the wall. But no - it was but a trick of the lights and the narrowness of the hall. She had moved into the room where Tricks would be lodging.

A musty smell rushed upon him as he entered. The room was so tiny that the three of them struggled to move about each other. This did little to lighten the ever-blackening sullenness of Rozalina. Pinnacle Tricks felt somewhat crestfallen, for the room of chilly and uninviting. He glanced at the ramshackle bed which lay below a window that had been left open.

"You must forgive us for the open window," begun Maria, "you see Maple; our cat oft frequents across the rooftops and likes to use this room as her threshold. You'll understand."

Tricks could do naught but sigh; it was not as if he had a choice. Yet Roza mercifully pulled the window shut and began to light a fire under the small stove. She then left the room, giving Tricks enough space to plonk his suitcase upon the bed and open it. Examining the room further, he moved to the pitcher and glass that sat on the bedside table.

"Ah! Water! You have my thanks. Running about this city has left me rather parched."

"Vodka." said Maria.

Tricks threw back the glass and instantly winced. For a moment it seemed he would expel the hearty drink back into the glass before his manners caught him and he swallowed with a struggle.

---

to be considered 'Gothic'.

[6] *Radcliffe:* Ann Radcliffe (1764–1823) British writer. Considered a pioneer of 'Gothic' literature. Famous works include *The Romance Of The Forest* (1791).

"Oh I see, uh, good. Quite good."

Maria smirked, "There is a tap there. And a pot for the stove there. I would boil the water before you drink it."

"Why would I need to do that? M-madam?" asked Tricks, but Maria had already left.

****

The room warmed by degrees. Pinnacle Tricks changed to his sleeping garments and stretched his weary feet out on the bed. He shivered vehemently in a vain attempt to warm the bed before he lay down to rest. There presently came a light rap on the door and Rozalina entered with a tray and a rare smile.

"Oh miss, why thank you!"

Roza placed the tray on the table and bowed sweetly as Tricks remembered that she did not speak English.

"Uh, spas-uh, spasibo."

"Ah, ochen khorosho.[7]" she smiled.

Tricks nodded vaguely.

"Borscht.[8]" Roza pointed at the tray.

"Borscht?"

"Da."

She smiled with a ghostly mystic that only compounded Tricks' uneasiness, but he was grateful for the hot soup after such an eventful evening. Rozalina left the man to his own devices and moved with haste to the reception, relieved that Maria had finally left for the night. And with the inn's only tenant fed and no doubt tired, she would hopefully be able to rest her mind for a few hours.

---

[7] *Oshen khorosho:* Russian – 'very fine'. The author has used Roman characters for Russian phrases – as such some minor errors may be present.

[8] *Borscht:* A soup consisting mainly of beetroot. A popular Russian dish.

III : The Journal of Pinnacle Tricks

"We rest; a dream has power to poison sleep. We rise; one wandering thought pollutes the day."

- Mary Shelley

How, I cannot say, but sleep is eluding me. My body aches with an exhaustion that is slowly dissipating into the warmth of this dismal little room. And invariably it is taking an incredibly long time to heat these quarters - surely such tiny confines would warm faster than this! There must be a draught from somewhere. I hear sounds - muffled and distant in the early pre-dawn. Someone must be cooking in this inn somewhere, for I hear a clanging of pots. Perhaps I could blame these noises for my lack of sleep, but that would be a falsity. The reality is my mind is hopelessly preoccupied. Here is to hoping that writing will tire me out enough; the sandman may come yet!

The soup was delicious; albeit strange - I am afraid I have already forgotten the name of it. I confess that I know little of Russian culture. I feel somewhat of a fool for the night's transpirations. Daft fool parading about a foreign city like a lost dog! I pray my embarrassed blushing was taken for a side effect of the cold. And of the cold - I hardly know where to begin describing it. Here I was thinking that we experienced cold winters on my fair British Isles but here, here! These Siberian winds are chilling to my very heart. Having been unable to summon a driver from Moscovsky Station, I consulted my map and deigned that I could reach the inn on foot. Herein lies the biggest mistake I've made thus far. Pray it is the worst; pray I don't get pneumonia! What a humiliating way to perish - *Here lies Tricks, the idiot who decided it would be a good idea to wander the icy streets!* - Bah! I long to be sent home. Fool that I am to have accepted this errand in the first place, but I fear to ignite the rage of Mr. Fairlie. He has made well aware of how expendable my position is, and fearing the wellbeing of my lovely wife Edythe, I wish not to leave her wanting for a home and lifestyle. There is no use in my complaining. My father oft reminded me about showing a little more servitude than asked for when it comes to work. My eyes grow heavy.

I must have dozed for a short spell; that restless sleep oft full of dreams that push towards nightmare possessed me. Consciousness allowed me to slip from its grasp several times, my eyes lingering on the waning gibbous outside my window that was beginning to set. And as that moon stared lovelessly - a sky's eye perhaps - from the shadows that crouched in every darkled corner there conjured violet horrors that set my exhausted heart into further exertion. Secreting from the cracks in the walls and floorboards these shadows crept in sinuous tendrils. From outside there came a shout of aggregation, most likely from some drunk stumbling through the street, yet his crude voice only added volume to my disquiet dreams, permeating through my ears like a sound underwater - muted and incoherent. The shadowy vines crept closer; such was their stealth that one barely noticed their movement. But still and tensed I lay as a wounded rodent in the striking range of a creeping serpent. A drip from the rusted faucet caused an involuntary lapse in my slumber where I raised my head drearily but for a moment. The shadows lay still - as those cast in a still room should do - and my subconscious reaffirmed that a dripping tap was no hazard to a sleeping man. Ready to plunge my head down onto the pillow once more I tensed suddenly; some shadow had moved but a fraction, moving with a spidery glide that paralysed my senses. Turning to the window I saw nothing out of the ordinary and surmised that it had been but a trick of my bleary eyes - an apparition conjured of slurred and sleepy sight. In and out of sleep I floated weightlessly - a cask in the sea of the dreamers - yet still I was not at ease. The dream sea was thick as oil and seemed to tarnish me with further poisonous terror. Again I imagined those icy tentacles of darkness seeping toward me and as I rolled over on the bed the glaring moonlight was on a sudden extinguished as a new shadow loomed over me. Feeling its cold, I awoke to see the moon gone, in its place the eldritch glow of green eyes boring into my very soul. I leapt awake with a start, stupefied by my fear, at the whim of whatever horrible creature belonged to those eyes. Stricken I fell from the bed, the icy touch of the floor confirming the reality of a beast in my sights, when the eyes shifted and what had been an elongated shadow shrunk into the proportions of a small cat. My heart raced with the residue of fear, yet relief had arrived by inches. It must be the cat that Maria had mentioned.

Damnable feline! Once again I embarrass myself. The cat had scraped at the window with a puppet string paw and beckoned me to open the window and let her in. Feeling a fleeting mercy for the thing trapped out in the cold I allowed her in; instantly she leapt onto the bed and sat rather expectantly on my pillow as if to inform that I was infringing on her property. *You may sleep on the floor* - her green eyes told me as such. I gave the thing a scratch under the chin and read the little medallion hanging from her collar. I recognised not some of those Cyrillic letters of the Russian alphabet but could discern that it must be the cat named Maple that I had been informed of.

By now the moon is beginning to set; I must concede that I will not sleep further this night. I am reminded of my younger days when insomnia was a regular occurrence; perhaps I will pass some time with the same recreations I would do in those times, but my drawing pencils are still packed away and I honestly cannot summon the energy. Instead I sit here, pen in hand, looking every now and then from my journal to the lightening sky outside the window. The pre-dawn glow lights up St. Isaac's Cathedral in magnificent fashion - that golden cap lustrously purging the night from its dome. I am told that it is near here that I will be meeting with a Mr. Dergatsya, who is to explain to me what Fairlie had so hurriedly skimmed over before ushering me on this expedition. I must say, I will need my coffee this morning if I've any chance of making sense of this whole ordeal! Pity the man who fails Fairlie - Lord may I not be that dullard!

IV : In the Office of Mr. Dergatsya

"No one can be happy in eternal solitude."

-    Anne Bronte

The sun that rose with the Petersburg morning was as sluggish with exhaustion as the city itself, gripped as it were with cold. Just as one struggles to rise from bed on a frigid morning, so too did the sunlight drag itself reluctantly over the spires of the cityscape. It offered little warmth, the bullying of cloud cover that benumbed its light left all beneath it hued with sombre greys. The morning groaned perfunctorily with the aches of the night's blizzard blows. The horses stamped; their masters stamped too in vain attempt to shrug the Arctic freeze from their appendages, as if to announce their recalcitrance towards the winter with defiance. These masters, just like their equine snorted mist from their mouths, while for some it was tobacco smoke. The snow that fell in gentle flakes clung to the streets in a bitter frost, whilst Petersburg fought back with the bellows of chimney smoke. The people would not yield; it was a new day and the show must go on. Storekeepers threw out their awnings, displayed their wares and the brave customers that strolled Nevsky Prospekt would be rewarded for such journeys away from their fireplaces.

Nestled betwixt two taller buildings, a small facade advertising hot beverages cried out for folk to enter its doors. Though this cry was hardly one of desperation - rather the cries were that of a busy shop, the kind where one might walk past and be unable to resist their own curiosity.

What hustle! Their wares must be of quality!

What bustle! Perhaps I should see what all the fuss is about?

Indeed, on such a day, a steaming coffee brought heartiness to the soul, and since it was too early for vodka and too late for tea, one fancied themselves deserving of the bitter strength of Italian espresso. Oh, Italy - That land of summer eternal! How much more does a man yearn for your impressionistic light[9] when the weather is so? If we could garner but the smallest taste of your summer in a single shot of espresso, we would sleep happily at night! And amongst the Russian locals that press themselves forcibly into the tiny shop, one would observe a small and wiry man cramped betwixt wall and table, gingerly consuming his prized coffee like a miser counting his gold; all the while writing in a small leather journal. Of what does he scribe? Is it his observations of Russia's cultural capital? Or perhaps a maudlin letter to a lover back home? Seems we are not to know – for he stood, excused himself to many a customer who pay him no mind, and he left the coffee shop in the direction of St. Isaac's Cathedral[10]. He was just another snow-crippled person moving through the city streets; and unless one were following him specifically, he would prove no more remarkable than any other who places their piece into the great jigsaw of Saint Petersburg. The man is of course, Mr. Pinnacle Tricks. The young Englishman, having revived himself from a restless slumber with coffee, moved through the streets with confidence. Though he knew not the lay of the city, the mighty gold dome of St. Isaac's guided him like a lighthouse beacon.

---

[9] *Impressionistic light:* Impressionism was an artistic movement made popular by French artists of the 19th century. The movement placed heavy emphasis on light, a theme that ties itself into this story.

[10] *St. Isaac's Cathedral:* Russian Orthodox Cathedral in Saint Petersburg. Completed in 1858.

****

On the second storey of a faceless building (faceless, one would say when compared to the opulence of St. Isaac's) across the road from the cathedral, a young woman sat and stared blankly. One might deride from her location that her gaze was enraptured by the beauty of the cathedral but no, she did not face the window. Instead she stared mindlessly at the wall of the office, stained with mildew, and awaited the arrival of the tardy Mr. Dergatsya[11]. The woman again wondered why she bothered to show up on time for work when her superior was always late. But then she pushed the thought away, for being well-versed as to how a day with Dergatsya played out, she remembered that this was the calmest she would be until she was dismissed at the end of the day. She rapped her fingernails beside the typewriter on her desk, the only noteworthy object in an otherwise cheerless room, sighed heavily and upon her exhale the door burst open and in charged a short man with an impressive moustache.

"Miss Povorot![12]"

"Sir,"

"You are at work?"

"Yes?"

"I had asked you the question, Missy! You know I dislike it when people confuse me!"

Here the man removed his felt hat and twirled on the spot looking for a place to put it. He furrowed his brow, looked to the floor and, seeing that there was snow on his boots, uttered a yawp before racing to the door scraper

---

[11] *Mr. Dergatsya:* The solicitor's name is a crude corruption of the Russian word meaning 'twitch' – an apt description of the man's personality.

[12] *Miss Povorot:* Again the name betrays the character; in this case a crude corruption of the Russian word meaning 'turn' – for she is constantly turning in and out of her superior's office.

and tapping his feet promptly. A short sigh exhumed from beneath his moustache before he was electrified into action again, remembering the hat clasped in his paw. By this point, Miss Povorot had arisen and moved to relieve him of his hat and coat, which she hung on the rack in next room. This room, being the office of Mr. Dergatsya, who indeed was the man who had just entered within, did little to lighten the dank feeling of the reception foyer but perhaps carried more character with its decor. Dergatsya muttered to himself as he followed Miss Povorot into the office; he sat at his desk, stood up and helped himself to a cup of water before ensconcing once more.

"Has he arrived yet?" he asked his secretary.

"The Englishman?"

"Who else, silly girl?"

"Who else is here but you and I?"

Dergatsya's face contorted with exertion and he appeared all at once flustered further, "Ooh! You sneaky witch! How enfeebled you perceive me! But of course I see he is not here yet!"

"But you asked the question." replied Miss Povorot.

"Y-you! You just return to your desk, woman!" he fumed.

Miss Povorot twirled and glided from the room. She had a grace to her movements that amplified her simple beauty. She was not a woman with whom men were wont to become instantly infatuated by, but there were subtleties in her gait, in the twist of her hair or the length of her neck. She had barely passed through the doorframe that separated the two rooms when she was once again summoned; Dergatsya sat perplexed as he struggled with his tie. His hands seemed too large for such a small man, and those meat hooks fumbled clumsily over one another.

"Confound this oppressive talisman!"

"May I, sir?"

Dergatsya handed Miss Povorot the tie, "My apologies Miss, my wife had made pies last night and I feel perhaps they are not agreeing with me at present."

"You just need your coffee." replied Miss Povorot, knotting tie on herself before handing it back to him.

"Indeed," mumbled Dergatsya.

Miss Povorot turned to leave before Dergatsya interjected again, "Ah miss? Did I ask you for my coffee?"

"No sir."

"Then I will do so now. You silly girl, you really should have suggested it to me."

The secretary sighed vexingly; upon returning to her desk she noticed a change in the bland room, for now a stranger stood in the centre. Miss Povorot felt her heart skip a beat, but when the man smiled to her in greeting she steadied herself. Despite his gaunt appearance, he looked friendly enough; she could only assume him to be the client awaiting Dergatsya.

"Tricks?"

The man nodded nervously, "Yes, uh, da! Da."

"I know little English." she said awkwardly.

"It is ok," replied Tricks, "Uh, Dergatsya?"

Here he pointed through the door to where Dergatsya had pressed his head against his desk and appeared to be weeping softly. Miss Povorot ushered Pinnacle into the office and the sobbing man gazed at him blankly.

"My shoes, Miss Povorot," he wept, "I cannot tie the laces. Confound it all! Confound it all!"

Pinnacle Tricks looked to Miss Povorot for guidance but she was no longer at his side.

"Uh, no sir. I am Pinnacle Tricks."

"Hmm? English? Tricks? Oh Tricks! But of course!"

He thrusted his hand forth and delivered a handshake so hardy it cramped Tricks' fingers.

Tricks winced; the hand he grasped was wet with tears and crushed his own emaciated fingers in its clutches. The pair sat as Miss Povorot entered with a tray of drinks.

"Goodness, Miss Povorot! Not now!" sniffed Dergatsya, wiping his face dry.

Povorot rolled her eyes in motion with her body as she spun about to leave the room.

"Oh, it is no trouble." said Tricks in an attempt to mediate the situation.

"It isn't? Miss Povorot! The coffee!"

Miss Povorot stormed back and slammed the tray onto the desk with impressive venom, but Mr Dergatsya paid no mind.

"Now then, now then," began Mr Dergatsya, before he paused, "Son; I must say it is rather bemusing. Bemusing, yes, that Mr. Fairlie would not make the journey himself on this occasion."

Pinnacle Tricks answered with his rehearsed response, "Mr. Fairlie is quite the busy man; I assure you though, that I am up to the task."

"Indeed. Well hopefully I can bring you up to speed on these affairs. My client is deceased; his final task for me was to ensure the wishes of his will were carried out in proper order."

"I am sorry for your loss, sir."

"Loss? Heavens boy, it is no issue for me. Merely an associate; I never met the man personally. A recluse, to be sure. Must have been an old comrade of your own Mr. Fairlie - the estate has been left in his name."

Mr. Tricks felt his eyebrows rise - though he shouldn't be so surprised, his boss had always been a secretive man of many hidden talents and eccentricities.

"Let's see here; 'Last will and testament of one Walpole Wight...'" muttered Dergatsya, "Article three - no that's not it. Ah! There!"

"The witness signature..." began Tricks.

Dergatsya interrupted, "A most curious enigma. The man had no known family. None that lived in any account. The will requested most of Wight's possessions be auctioned. However, the estate was left in the name of one Ereven Fairlie with a note that it was 'something that you would want belonging to you.'"

"Yes," added Tricks, "but the witness signature."

"A befuddling head-scratcher, but not one that -"

"Sir, please!" interrupted Tricks, "Who is this person who signed witness?"

Dergatsya squinted and placed the paper beneath his nose, "Why young man, I do not know. I hadn't paid much attention."

Scribbled with a penmanship that resembled that of a child, the name 'Leaf' had been scrawled as witness.

"Surely that is not someone's name? A patronym? A surname?" asked Dergatsya, as though he expected Tricks to have the answer. Pinnacle Tricks could only shrug.

"Either way, we've no contact on Wight's estate. As such you will need to go there and claim the keys yourself. On behalf of Mr. Fairlie, of course. The deeds should be within those halls somewhere."

Tricks felt his heart skip a beat, "The estate is local?"

"My no! Lapland![13]"

"L-Lapland?" Tricks felt weak at the knees, "But how am I supposed to -"

"Here sir."

Mr. Dergatsya spun the small globe on his desk and thrust his meaty finger over a region of Scandinavia. Pinnacle Tricks choked on his speech; surely there had to be some mistake.

"But the deeds are not here? I am due to begin my return to England on the morrow!"

"The deeds, sir, are within the house. And I hardly believe the deceased is ready to march his way down to Petersburg to deliver us the keys, eh what?"

Mr. Tricks sighed, "It is only that my wife will be expecting me home."

"A married man! Well then I am sure it will be a handsome pay check coming home with you in a few weeks' time!"

---

[13] *Lapland:* Region in Finland.

"A few weeks?!" cried Tricks.

"There, there lad. I hardly see how that is my problem. Fear not, I hear it is a lovely place."

Pinnacle Tricks was dumbfounded, "But I've no ticket, no reservations - I don't speak your native language!"

"Oh yes!" here Dergatsya clicked his fingers.

As if from nowhere there entered a stout man in a bedraggled overcoat. Given the appearance of his eyes, sunken as they were in darkened pouches, Tricks was given quite a start by the gentleman. His hair wisped above his head in but a few stray feathers, though despite having every likeness of a man escaped from an asylum his face had certain warmth to it.

"When you leave tomorrow this man will be your guide," Mr. Dergatsya stood to greet him, "He speaks excellent English."

The man bobbed in a polite bow, "Very good to meet you, Mr. Tricks."

Tricks stood to shake his hand, "And you too. My, your speech is impeccable, Mr - uh?"

The man spoke his name just as Mr. Dergatsya let out an almighty sneeze. The translator began again, and although Pinnacle Tricks strained to gather the collection of Cyrillic syllables he still did not understand. As he spoke again, from outside a crow cawed, Miss Povorot upset a pitcher of water on the desk, and still Tricks did not catch the name. Despite Mr Tricks' increasingly blushed face, the mystery man showed no signs of impatience.

"Perhaps," said the stranger, "You may just refer to me as Viy.[14]"

"Viy?"

"Viy."

"Viy!" blurted Mr. Dergatsya, "There he goes again!

---

[14] *Viy:* Perhaps the most famous horror story of Nikolai Vasilievich Gogol (from *Mirgorod*, 1835).

Too many books, good sir! Such a waste of time. Who is it now?"

Viy pleaded earnestly, "My good man, it is Gogol!"

"It is ridiculous is what it is!" huffed Dergatsya, "If you spent as much time at work as you do reading you might have achieved something more prestigious!"

Viy gave no heed to the insult, instead shaking Pinnacle's hand and giving him a friendly wink. Pinnacle Tricks' hand may as well have been a dead fish; he stood agog at what had just transpired. Had Fairlie known of this? Was he really expected to venture further afield? With no swift way of contacting his boss, Mr. Tricks had no choice but to follow the orders given to him. There was no way he could return to London without this matter settled, his job depended on it. Not that Mr. Dergatsya cared. The flippant man had returned to his desk and, as if assuming himself alone in the office he procured a small pocket mirror and began combing his impressive moustache. Viy stood at Pinnacle's side, grinning with an unsettling simplicity; soon Miss Povorot entered and offered egress to the two gentlemen. With the door slammed behind them faster than one could think, Viy and Tricks were alone on the cold Petersburg street, the bells of the cathedral toiling above them. The black birds that had settled in the bare trees that lined the street all called their response to the bell, scattering like dark hailstones with the beat of inky wings. Tricks flinched as the birds swooped near him, while Viy grasped his shoulder and said with a friendly grin, "I will pick you up tomorrow. Be ready."

Thereupon Viy left with a hunched and purposeful stride, while the black birds flew off into the sun that set over the construction of the Church on Spilled Blood.[15]

---

[15] *The Church On Spilled Blood:* This famously colourful church is an icon of Saint Petersburg, currently under construction at the time of this story.

V : Viy

"Why does the wind whirl in the gully whipping up leaves and clouds of dust when ships becalmed upon the ocean impatiently await its breath? Why does an eagle, mighty, fearsome, fly from the crags past lofty towers to a rotten tree stump? Ask him, then! So too a poet: like a gale he gathers anything he wants; he flies, like the eagle, where he will; and asking no one for permission, like Desdemona, he insists on choosing the object of his love."

- Alexander Pushkin

The man named Viy, for there were far too many challenges in labelling him under his Christian name, could have been excused for emanating a bewilderment similarly felt by his latest acquaintance. Unlike Pinnacle Tricks however, he strolled rather jauntily away from the office of Mr. Dergatsya, the Petersburg twilight glowing weakly on his rosy countenance. The steady rhythm of his untroubled composure echoed through his short and crisp steps, and although the prospect of a daunting journey hung about his person like so many vampire bats, he stood tall with a confidence that could have been mistaken for naivety. A tune whistled past his lips, as though the cold wind that blew across his unfortunately balding head were little more than an afterthought, and the black birds soaring noisily above him would shield him from the night's chill. Yet even he knew the importance of retiring before the turned dark; with the days so short and weather so uncompromising at that time of year, one felt the pulse of their step increase whilst wandering from place to place. A door nondescript from any other would mark the entrance to his destination; just another gateway on a nondescript laneway branching from Nevsky Prospekt.

Viy patiently stamped the snow from his boots and advanced up the creaking stairs. His home was one of unpretentious pleasures, and the crossing of the threshold split his world into a paradoxical paradise. The colours changed; on a sudden the dreary blues and uninviting violets gave way to an impressionistic clime of warm orange and burnt sepia. A fire crackled cheerfully, illuminating in a soft light the homely contours of Viy's crumbled loft. The books, of which there were so many as to dominate the cramped quarters, piled themselves around in a fashion both orderly and chaotic. Serving purposes other than that of being read, these tomes propped open doors, balanced empty coffee cups on their hard-bound surfaces, and pressed between their musty pages the butterflies and flowers from a long-forgotten summer. Their many dusty leaves were dog-eared here and bookmarked there; it appeared that none had been finished, as Viy was someone who always took on a bit more than could be expected from one man, and these half-read books invariably illustrated a physical metaphor of their owner's distracted existence. In fact Viy would ignore all else in his home, his attention arrested by a fluttering that thumped against his window. The shutter was flung open, the air that poured into the room was unforgivingly icy, and the walls seemingly shivered at its presence. Viy stared at the tawny owl that had huddled for warmth on his sill. Yet even this bird could not retain the man's gaze, for he would then survey his home and ponder somewhat belatedly the pleasures that dwelt with him. How was it that the world of twilit comforts could exist so obliviously separated from the cold by inches of wood and stone? Two sides of the same coin; a planet spinning on its axis with one half dozing lazily with blood warmed while the other side shivers bleakly with the cutting moonlight - such imagery compared the orange glow of Viy's humble home to the wicked night cloaking its winter against the outside facade. The icy nettles on his coat softened; he stiffly adjusted the storm-tousled wisps of his hair and sighed deeply, taking for himself one morsel of his inviting home and its familiar smells before returning his gaze to the bird.

"Hello Owl. Will you be sharing again your tawny down? Might I pluck thee of a single plume to fashion as my quill? Will thee, in doing as such, dip thy talons into the ink of philosophy and assist the forming of my ideas with a thoughtful scratching? Would thee convict me of plagiarism were I to preserve my ideas with *your* pen?[16]"

A voice came from behind him, "Silly man. Close that window! You would allow the cold to kill us both for the sake of this bird?"

Viy's countenance was visibly lifted at the arrival of this voice, and he turned his head to look upon his wife. Stoic and gentle, there was within her stout frame a loving authority that Viy could not help but devote himself to. That he was flippant has already been established; too many thoughts cluttered his mind, so much that even his wife struggled to steal his attention. Yet it is said that the heart cries louder than the mind, and her very arrival could erase all her husband's many passions in a single stroke and arrest him completely.

"Wife; my heart is yours alone, but my brain is with the birds."

"You can say that again."

"You are troubled."

"You are leaving."

"To the north."

"You would break my heart by leaving? At the very least you submit your own; at the very least I then possess a spare."

---

[16] *Hello Owl…:* Viy's somewhat sudden eloquence comes from him speaking his native language. The previous chapter saw him speaking English, and may have outlined him as less educated than he appears now.

"Humourous woman!" he continued, "While it must be that I quit this abode but temporarily, my heart remains here with you. And how can a man continue so long without the beat of a heart?"

Although she tried to retain an air of good humour, her eyes swelled with tears that struck Viy down to his most base form, and he could do nothing else but rush to his wife and clasp her in the confines of embrace.

"Good woman! I redouble my devotion! Perish any thought of my absence being permanent - or long, for that matter! I return in a few days.[17]"

"Foolish man to leave your wife for even a day!"

Viy searched for a way to stem the rivulets of tears that twined through his wife's wrinkled face.

"I take my ring, bound to my finger - let it be to me another vital appendage!"

Here he raised in his hand an aged rose gold ring, glistening under the lamp light.

"Let it be a constant reminder of the Lord's blessing. You! You are that blessing. And I shall ache for you this entire duration of my sojourn and bring home for you a healthy pay and presents of the tundra."

"You promise many things. All I wish is you returned in safety."

"And return I shall, wreathing your silver hair with festoons of ivy, adorning your antiquated beauty with roses."

"Silly man. Come, let us eat."

Closing the window without another thought towards the owl, and caring not about the stack of tomes that was knocked over as he advanced across the floor, Viy followed his wife to their table. Their bones creaked as they sat; their old furniture groaned under their elbows;

---

[17] *Good woman!...:* This loving converse between Viy and his wife echoes Gogol's short story *The Old World Landowners* (from *Mirgorod*, 1835).

outside the facade of their home struggled with the howling wind. But these creaks and groans were far from the tortured agonies one might associate with such words. It was these sounds that echoed with the pulse of life and filled the happy couple with the comfort felt by one who stretches their body in their sleep. His finely trimmed beard became bedraggled with flecks of meat and cabbage as he ate, yet that night Viy would not think again of the adventure ahead of him. Truly blessed as he was with clarity, he instead stared lovingly at his wife, who smiled back at him with all the loveliness of a portrait that Viy could lock into his mind for safekeeping, referring to it when his journey may seem too difficult and he would yearn for the very moment in which he was now enraptured.

VI : The Journal of Pinnacle Tricks
Lapland, 1888

"There is no greater sorrow than to recall our times of joy in wretchedness."

- Dante Alighieri

That meeting with Mr. Dergatsya would be a prelude to the rather disquiet few days that would follow. Upon my return to the inn I would discover that blasted cat had shed an awful amount of hair on my already dismal bed, and as such I had no choice but to spend a cheerless night in that room sneezing profusely. The man Viy was true to his word, that mysterious fellow arriving before dawn with a horses and trap prepared. Had I known what sort of journey awaited me, I might have snuck quietly out the back door of the inn and made my nameless escape back to England - damn the consequences. But I shamefully digress; I am not such a renegade as I am unabashedly dutiful. The good book encourages the man who suffers for doing good. But the grisly winter that has settled on this land has left me doubting my countenance. May I be filled with vigour anew.

Rozalina generously equipped us with copious stores for our journey. Only it would appear that most of the foods she bestowed were merely those that were not devoured the day before. We could only appreciate these gifts. Our trap, which offered only minor shelter from the elements, was burdened to brim with wares. Viy had seen to the provision of tents, a small stove and other necessities, so that there was very little space for the two of us to sit alongside. He would greet me by slapping one of those Russian hats atop my brow - the very same I mentioned in an earlier passage - the warmth it brought came alongside a style that I think my wife will enjoy as a souvenir. My initial doubts at the stamina of those two small horses tasked with hauling us along were abated swiftly as we commenced. They trotted with the regality of stallions, and the sunrise reflecting sweetly from the surface of the frozen Neva River as we crossed was exceptional. Those pink rays gave minimal warmth yet played wonderfully with the cold tones of a watery city gripped by winter. One could not help but be reminded of stories of northern lights[18], of auroras - was this a sight that could rival their phenomenon? The lamps had dwindled to a weak smoulder, though the dawn gave as much light as we needed to proceed. Around us, Petersburg slowly rose from its shivering slumber, and it was at this moment that I at last felt a small amount of contentment. Such beauty spilling from the eastern sky made me think of Edythe, and the homesickness that ensued was accentuated by the cool air. I must admit I am not one for such a disrupted life; my heart yearns rather pathetically for home and its comforts, remaining reluctantly aware of the responsibilities that come with my station. Oh my Edythe, how understanding she had been when I informed her of this damnable quest. How I wish I could have taken her with me.

The canals and roadways of Saint Petersburg would very soon give way to a bleak landscape. It was flat and featureless, spotted here and there with ramshackle cottages and ill-tended pastures; a country in hibernation, the frozen millponds sealing whatever life sustained beneath ice. The wheels of windmills stood static - the gale would not move them, for it blew upon them a frost that held them fast. It was this water-logged countryside that

---

[18] *Aurora Borealis:* Light phenomena observed at night in Northern latitudes. This mention continues the theme of 'ghost lights' populating the story.

led me to recall the words of Coleridge[19], for there was indeed water everywhere! Yet who would want to partake in this cheerless scene? I felt for the poor citizens who made their lodgings in those dismal shacks, until Viy informed me that most of them would be in disuse until the summertime. It was for this reason that no train could carry us to our destination, for the infrequent nature of the population would not sustain such transport.

He would go on to tell me of his life, and it was at this point I begged inwardly that he would again divulge to me his proper title; now that we were alone in this vast quiet I had no doubt that I might have actually comprehended his name. Alas it is now too late - I am too invested in the new friendship, but fortunately 'Viy' remained the only utterance he used to address himself. His story covered the years as our trap did cover the miles, and having had such a unique life I feel it necessary to detail it here in this journal; albeit I daresay in brief.

Having been born of poverty in the ashes of Moscow's great fire[20], Viy would very much (in terms of dignity) personify the rising of phoenix, for he displayed an intelligence that conflicted with his lowly position (I must admit I feel such an ape to refer to such a charismatic gentleman as such). Through means that he as a child could not recall, his parents had perished, and Viy had ended up leaving his beloved Russia and found himself in my home of Britain. A page boy to some member of higher echelon, Viy had been taught of English language, a

---

[19] *Recall the words of Coleridge: Rime Of The Ancient Mariner* (1798) – famous work of British poet Samuel Taylor Coleridge (1772–1834). There is irony in Tricks' comparison of the poem to the surrounding landscape; the verse in question describes a thirst-stricken ship crew lost at sea under a hot sun – unlike the water-rich surroundings of Lapland.
[20] *Fire of Moscow:* In this sense not literal. Moscow suffered from a great fire at the hands of Napoleon Bonaparte's army in 1812, around the time that Viy would have been born.

feat I find impressive given the conflicting differences
between it and that of Russian tongue. Under the tutelage
of his compassionate benefactor, Viy had access to many
great books from his master's library. He would grow to
love reading; despite his already whimsical situation he oft
found himself delving into the daydream worlds of his
favourite fiction. Perhaps it was this nostalgic reverie that
had led him to wish for a return to his home country upon
adulthood, a request reluctantly granted by his benefactor,
who at this point considered the lad to be his own. Upon
his return, he would find Russia to be changed greatly.
Despite the drastic step down the social ladder that such a
move had permitted - namely moving from the page of a
rich Londoner to an anonymous Russian in the streets of
Moscow - Viy vehemently admitted his preference to his
homeland, regarding his fortuitous upbringing as a
blessing, but not where he was called to remain.

Viy would have happily spent his remaining years in
Moscow, until, as always, the life requirement of work and
reimbursement called, hence why he had begun working as
a translator. He would easily admit to his reluctance to
travel due to these reasons. There was something very
monk-like in his persona.

It would occur to me only then that I had not inquired
as to our destination. Though I knew us to be bound to
some place in that vast taiga of Scandinavia, the specifics
of the trip had been lost in the rabble of its rapidity. What
shock I would receive to hear that Viy had no knowledge
of our destination, merely its location marked on a dirty
old map. Procuring it from his coat for me to observe, I
felt instantly awed - my position as but one tiny speck on
this vast world overcame me completely. The map was
incomplete; a hurried scribble of Finland's curved coast,
where Saint Petersburg nestled in the gulf betwixt it and
the Baltics. This was not some relic of old centuries, where
the world's end usually warned that 'here be-eth dragons' -
this age we live in is one far more civilised. But I could not

help but be swamped by the endless waves of forest that surrounded us as we delved deeper in that wintery Thule. And indeed the trees seemed to creep closer as we rumbled along. As we crawled onward I would be grateful for these trees, as they shielded our roadway somewhat from any excessive drifts that might impede our progress. This however, would not stop those mischievous ravens from sabotaging our path; the birds swooping ahead of us, landing on branches above that would dump snow onto the road or - heaven forbid - our cart. Curse the things!

We had little choice but to set up camp on the roadside, and to say I had an utmost cheerless night sleep would be an understatement. My weariness increases with each day that I am away from home. I daresay I have not had a restful sleep since I left London. If nothing else I found cheer in good food and drink; Viy baking a simple bread over our humble little fire, this accompanied by a wonderfully hearty drink called 'crass'[21]. The following day would contain much of the same; the forest encroached, the road unrolled steadily before us. The water-logged terrain had not abated with the increasing trees; the ponds of sludge-ice that dotted the fields soon turned into full blown lakes, and the chilled wind that crept all around and into one's bones seemed to whisper good riddance. Our position as warm-blooded men in this harsh land left us feeling discomfort. The scenery maintained its sombre beauty. The pines jutted roughly from the banks, and where the ice had broken into those little pancake-shaped discs, I could observe the queerest of lights darting about the water's surface. Such bizarre little lanterns! Surely this clime was too frigid for fireflies. Viy, in his admirable wisdom, told me that they were ghost lights. Ignis Fatuus, or Will-O-The-Wisp. Such expressions I had not heard before, yet they no doubt instilled a sense of uneasiness in

---

[21] *Crass:* Tricks means *kvass,* a fermented beverage popular in Eastern Europe. He has dictated the word phonetically.

my composure. I found myself thinking of the stories of my childhood, of ghastly figures such as Halloween Jack and Rawhead-and-Bloodybones[22]. We were in the company of Paasselkä Devils[23], Viy had explained. The 'faeries' played tricks on travellers, taunting them with an eerie luminance, encouraging them to veer from the path and into the lakes. I shudder to think of the fools that might lie beneath the ice in watery graves; thankfully I had the company of such a fine raconteur who could keep me on course!

We would at last reach our destination as the sun set on the third day; my bewilderment mounted with the days, and the mystery surrounding this unusual errand proliferated. Plaguing me above all other questions - why had Mr. Wight, a presumably English man, seen fit to conceal himself in this far stretch of isolated terrain? I thought of this Mr. Wight, the life he must have led, the ties that bound him to my superior and the details of his bizarre position. These unnerving thoughts plunged me into a fear I could not describe upon reaching the town that Wight had called home. What greeted us was not a bustling mountain townage I had expected. No, what appeared before us was far more sinister. The town was deserted.

---

[22] *Rawhead-and-Bloodybones:* A bogeyman of English folklore created to frighten naughty children.
[23] *Paasselkä Devils:* A will-o-the-wisp; light phenomena appearing over certain Finnish lake regions.

45

VII : Letter from Leaf

"Who has seen the wind? Neither you nor I: but when the trees bow their head, the wind is passing by."

-   Christina Rossetti

Dear Mother,

I saw you again but you didn't wave.

Thorn is being mean to me. She is such a nasty sister. Just because she is a few minutes older she thinks she can treat me badly. I think she wants you all to herself. Oh Mother, say it isn't true that you two dance in the moonlight without me!

Papa is gone, but Papa is mean, too. Thorn told me Papa isn't around anymore and he isn't. I thought I saw Papa but Thorn said I didn't. I thought I saw Papa the same way I see you Mother, in my dreams in my dreams. In my dreams there you are and there is Papa sometimes too but Thorn said that you are just a ghost. Papa used to say you were a ghost too but now he is also a ghost and I saw him. You used to live with us, Mother; Papa and Thorn said so, but how can Thorn know that when we are twins? I believed Papa though - he said you went away when I was a baby but I see you so you can't have gone too far.

Thorn is not so bad. She gave me a 'paisley'. I love my 'paisley' it is green and looks like a tear. I put it on a string around my neck. I hold it when I'm worried and I'm worried that we might have to leave home now that Papa is gone. Thorn says don't be stupid and I tell her she is stupid. I am still worried though.

It is always cold when you appear in my dreams, so cold that I always wake up shivering and my tears are sticky on my face. Then comes the dry; I feel so dry like a LEAF shrivelling in the wind and it doesn't go away for a long time. But I try not to be awake when you appear in my dream because I just want to stay asleep because I just want to see you for as long as I can. This time you were dancing and you saw me and you cried and your tears were icicles and the blood ran from your eyes and onto your face and dress. But you were still so beautiful Mother with the red on your face when all else was blue. I feel so certain that you are alive when I see the blood and it melts the ice, the only heat in my frozen dreamlands. You can't be gone. I don't believe it.

Dear mother, I've seen you so many times but you never speak to me. My other letters are always there when I go back; do you read them and then leave them there? I always see the white of the paper under the rock when I get there and I cry because nobody tells me anything and I just want to be with you.

Last night was a dream and the moon was going to fall and we only had three days to dance under it before it would consume us and you saw me bleeding, bleeding until my heart was dry.

I miss you.

I miss you.

I miss.

Leaf.

VIII : The Journal of Pinnacle Tricks
"All partings foreshadow the great final one."
-     Charles Dickens

The town, were it even large enough to be titled as such,
could have been easily dismissed as some abandoned
settlement had it not been for the obvious traces of
sophistication that lay in shambles in its streets. Indeed the
many buildings brought to mind Gaudi's neo-gothic
influences[24] [25], which complemented the archaic ruin that
comes with abandonment; yet these facades would no
doubt compliment nature's serpent of decay - the ivy vine -
that had overgrown in shoots about its long dead prey.
The lamps stood tall with crooked claw reaching, as
though they wished to dip into the sun like a bucket in a
well, and draw forth a tiny morsel of heat and energy. The
ground beneath the town seemingly ruptured with the
blows of an unseen titan, bursting forth root and sediment
onto the scattering cobblestones, making a difficult
passage for any horse and carriage hoping to pass through.
But the acrid scent of death hung in the air, and any
travellers foolish enough to plunge so far into the taiga
would need little to convince them of pursuing another
route. That most eldritch of sights was saved for the
darkled estate that perched itself above the town like an
eagle guarding its nest. It crippled the hillside with its

---

[24] *Gaudi:* Antoni Gaudi (1852–1926) Spanish Catalan
architect who popularised the Modernisme architectural
movement.
[25] *Neo-Gothic:* Also Victorian Gothic. Architectural
movement centred mainly in England.

presence, from the rusted gates up the bleak path to the ghastly summit. The trees surrounding - so green as to almost be black - guarded the house with otherworldly sentience, their claw-like protuberances reminiscent of enormous undead arms reaching from the lair of Dis[26].

It was this estate that would be my destination. The sight of that sickly place evoked dread when I had expected relief. Relief? Was that the correct word? After the crippling journey away from the comforts of home, who could say what I can look forward to. Our caravan could peruse the streets no further. How ironic - that the terrain of this humane civilisation would prove more impassable that the dense forest from whence we'd come. Trees lay fallen across the roads and the dirty snow coated the place with a sickly ensemble. Who could call this home? Furthermore - and perhaps the most pressing issue - was there anybody here? I turned to Viy as if to confirm whether we had found the correct place, however he could only stare back at me with the same puzzlement. We must have misinterpreted the map. That could be the only logical explanation. Yes, this could not be the town we had set out for; this could only be some settlement that had long since been erased from the globe. Viy, as jaunty as you like, casually rolled himself a cigarette and asked, "What's your plan?" I can't say I cared much for this remark, but I endevoured to remember this man was my guide and what felt like the only other human being on the face of the Earth! I asked him was he certain that this was our destination. As if pre-empting my question, he swiftly procured the map and tapped his stubby finger upon it. There was no denying it - this must be the place. My heart sank with the burden of worriment. My nonchalant companion would guide my thoughts in the correct

---

[26] *Dis:* The name of the fictional city in Dante Alighieri's *Inferno* (1320). *Dis Pater (Father Dis)* is described in Roman mythology as 'ruler of the underworld.'

direction, asking me if I would like him to inquire about for an inn. While I ached from our journey, I could hardly allow him to go alone; as such I offered to join him in the search. But he would resolutely deny my assistance, suggesting I remain with the coach and our supplies in case of bandits. He was gone before I could protest that the caravan was pretty much defenceless with or without my guarding it, and I was left alone in this hideous settlement.

He was gone far longer than I anticipated. I watched the sky transitioning into a night where the cool light of the moon threw charlatan shadows, morphing the most mundane of objects into twisted minstrels of the macabre. The silence grew - thick, as encompassing as the ocean floor, accentuating the foreboding sense of gloom strewn about the air like sticky cobwebs coating skeletal tree branches.

Evanescent wisps of cloud flitted across the stony sky at speeds faster than would be expected for this otherwise still surrounding. My foreboding sense of isolation was exaggerated by the quiet; finding my lodgings became my only ambition. An infantile instinct could not shake the thought that I was being watched. Despite the dark shadows providing more than adequate concealment from any unseen predators lurking in the gloom, the fronds of cold air draped across my shoulders seemed to expose my being as one of heat and pulse, so blatantly opposite to what could be expected of this locale. Surely by my being the only living thing in this ghost town of dead men left me passively exposed. Perhaps it was mere paranoia, but I knew then that I had to find Viy. I could wait no longer for his re-emergence. And so I steeled myself; a clear path of logical action beginning to weave itself together in my mind. I rose from my post and wandered several steps before realising I could not recall the direction that Viy had taken. Lucky left, I decided. Recalling the old iteration I used as a child galvanised my resolve, albeit slightly.

Perhaps since I was born *gauche* (in both handedness and the other unfortunate definition of the word)[27] I found it a favourable notion of choosing left instead of its opposite, and it was left I went at the first available fork in the cobblestone path at my quivering feet. The dusk was only just sharp enough to cut away shadows of loose and treacherous stones that may have tripped me up otherwise. Tentative steps soon turned to a light trot. As my vision became clearer I felt inclined to pick up my pace for a few metres before coming to a sudden stop. Gazing skyward, the starless canvas of water-coloured grey seemed to suggest the currents of frigid gale silently racing across the shivering cosmos. These winds, at such high altitudes, streaked like brushstrokes down to the borders of distant pines to portray a dome in which I was indefinitely trapped; a soldier of snow held static within a glass globe. My head ached as my sight was averted from the glow of the rising moon. And then, as if forgetting why I had ceased to run in the first place, I jogged forward again, my pace quickening with each heavy footfall of my shoes. My heels pressed so hard into the ground in rhythm to the sickening thump of my threadbare heart; the pressure of those weighted steps seemed to push more air out of my burning lungs, stuffed as they were from irregular and fear-laden breaths. *Where was Viy?*

By then the night had fallen. Tunnel vision ensued and as I pressed onward the repetition of cobblestone under foot lulled me into a hypnotic countenance that was broken on sudden by a most terrifying spectre. A phantom, undeniably effeminate in shape, stood in the umbra of a haggard and bare tree shadow, shielded from the light of the moon.

---

[27] *Gauche:* French – can be used for 'left' (as in left-handedness) or 'graceless'. Here Pinnacle degrades himself for comedic effect, perhaps to dispel the tension of his situation.

Perhaps my senses were sharpened by the ominous foreboding that plagued my being, for I was able to discern the being from some twenty metres distant. It seemed to face me, as I stood paralysed in the open and revealing moonlight, staring right back through eyes dripping with terror. I cannot recall how long I stood motionless there, unable to clear my clouded head or move any muscle. How I remained standing through such dread I still find unbelievable, as I distinctly remember the rush of pallor draining from my face.

Nothing would come of nothing[28] - the words of some fictional king appeared before my mind's eye, for what reason I did not know. I had to react to this ghostly being, be it through interaction or fleeing in unrestrained dismay. Once again a logical rendition descended upon me, and, dismissing such ghouls as absurd, chose upon calling out to the apparition, inquiring about the absence of the populace of this dreadful village. Cold fear choked my words as I tried to speak; I was somehow able to croak a timorous "Hello" in the direction of the shadowy figure. Only my voice betrayed my unease, for I remained steadfast of stance, my eyes fixed boldly on this other being against all instinctual desire to run away in cowardice. The dark ghost seemed to consider my acknowledgement a moment, before its most eldritch response. Stirring from its standstill, the dusky humanoid turned its body and in three steps walked slowly to my right, slipping out of view behind a grey stone building, never leaving the shadow of the tree in which it stood, never arresting its gaze from my direction. It was at this moment my fear descended yet another rung closer to madness; a frightening groan that sounded utterly inhumane escaped my parched lips. I gave my surroundings a quick glance and then, feverish with panic,

---

[28] *'Nothing would come of nothing':* Alludes to William Shakespeare's *King Lear* (1606)

I crept forward slowly and as soundlessly as I could muster in the direction of the ruins. The sharp staccato of my breathing betrayed me; futilely trying to remain undisclosed to this otherworldly being.

The building loomed closer, in mere steps I would be upon it. But then what? To peer around the corner from whence the ghost disappeared - what was it I possibly hoped to see? The coward within prayed I would observe nothing, but as to whether that meant the fiend was very real and had disappeared or was a mere fragment of the overworked imagination I would never know. Childish flights of fancy swam in the sick waters of my migraine, my pulse throbbing loudly in my ears. Past a blackened doorway in the facade I sidled, not daring to turn my gaze into the void within. I shivered to place my fingertips upon its rough stone surface, and with one more step and all the willpower I had left I peered slowly around the corner. With a reaction that impeded my senses yet again, I stood and stared at nothing; for nothing, at least of the fantastic and supernatural countenance, was present before me. Long, dried grass overgrown around more twisted trees and broken footpath. Another anguished cry was wrenched from my mouth. Had I seen anything tangible? Could this apparition be nothing more but the hallucinations of a madman? Again the child within emerged dominant, stronger than before, and I desperately wanted to hide. Hide and squeeze my eyes shut tight until I awoke from this terrible dreamland. Carelessly, I turned about face and hastily stepped into the inky darkness beyond the building entrance. Then, frightening my heart to a standstill - the deafening cry of a crow I had disturbed with my entering; my eyes plunged into further blackness by the plumage of my frantic companion. With a caw almost as terrified as my own, the crow flew from the ruins and disappeared into the distant trees. My heart throbbed violently; I felt as though the abandoned thing would burst from its rib cage, throwing itself at anything or anyone that might show me compassion in this isolated purgatory. Oh Gods, how alone I felt at that moment!

I found myself sinking to my haunches, back pressed against the loveless walls of this gutted building trying to dampen the sobs that I involuntarily convulsed. Only by the most astonishing power of my will - power which I did not know I possessed - was I soon able to venture back out onto the street. There was little I could do now but return to the coach. Morning would bring with it clarity and the light to search for this town's somehow absent populace. Call me a coward if you will, but after seeing such a frightening spectre I had little problem with huddling in the caravan until sunrise. My mind and feet ticked over mechanically, as though shielding my higher consciousness from any further damage; I walked for what felt like hours when it was more likely mere minutes. When I rounded the corner that finally brought the caravan into view, I was met with a relieving if not puzzling sight. Crouched around a small fire was Viy, tending to his iron coffee pot while wisps of cigarette smoke coiled sinuously about his person. Relieved almost to the point of tears I greeted him, yet it was not long before suspicions crept in and I had to inquire to where he had disappeared to. He would beat me to it though, stating that there was not a soul to be found and that perhaps we should inquire directly at the estate. I wondered whether I should tell him about that hideous shadow; I shuddered involuntarily to think of it. Viy seemed to share my uneasiness, saying that the entirety of this ghost town felt tainted, *cursed.*

IX – The Dryads

"The darker the night, the brighter the stars, the deeper the grief, the closer is God!"

-       Fyodor Dostoyevsky

On the other side of the village, espied earlier by Pinnacle Tricks, stood the hideous house on the hill - Wight Estate. The estate was of sickly dimensions, a hollow tower rising emaciated from its squat entrance, the gust-struck atrium echoing within. The stone stairs of the threshold gripped with tree root tenacity, and as a flame dwindles the further it flies from its core, the tower quivered weakly in the wind. Were one to follow a gust on its fleeting race, they could fly up dampened steps and whistle through the keyhole to where a staircase wraps its viper steps around the atrium for three uneven floors. From an open window on the third floor a shutter was thrown violently open, and a young woman could be seen hurling some small object from the sill. The girl took a moment to wipe her weeping face with her emaciated arm before struggling with the wind to close the shutter. Cut off from grey glare of the awful day the girl shivered in the darkness, taking a moment to allow her sight to adjust to the light of a dying fire burning sadly in the hearth. Her sobs were wretched, causing her sallow eyes to sting and her raw-boned ribs to convulse. She was Ague Wight, daughter of the recently deceased Warpole. While it would seem natural for the girl to be crying given the loss of her father, the melancholia that seized her was rather native to her person, and this episode of grief was none too dissimilar to any other day lost in the drowning waves of her crippled sanity. With a temperament so infantile, she appeared both physically and mentally younger than her five and twenty years could tell, and as she peered through the swathes of messy curls at the fire before her she fell into a calm trance. Ague seemed permanently drained of all pallor, as though she had never been taught of spectral light beyond that of monochrome; her hair was of such washed out brown that it could almost be grey, while the pale skin was blemished with the sickly colour of old porridge. Benumbed she sat, a forgotten project of an absent deity, left to gather the dust of senility on her brow, the fire and wind of her surroundings muttering about their business.

What had upset her so? What thought had ignited such fury? A groan louder than that of the wind pierced her daydream; the door of the small room creaked ajar. Ague ignored this intrusion and therein stepped a doppelganger of improved appearance - her twin sister Hemlocke. Although she shared similar features to her twin, her figure was fuller and less malnourished, face of warmer pallor and there was more order in the dark curls of her hair. Were Ague to gaze into a mirror that reflected the best possible order of her features, the image would have been not unlike her sister. That was not to say that Hemlocke was any better off for her beauty, for her countenance bore a perpetual frown, the edges of her mouth drawn down with the weight of a tumultuous existence fraught with perplexity.

"Are you still crying?"

Ague peered up from the fire, "Horrible Thorn. Pointy sister."

"I told you to stop calling me that, Ague."

"Horrible…"

Hemlocke approached her sister and tenderly smoothed her hair out of her face, with the recipient showing childish resistance.

"Here, you have gotten yourself dirty again."

"I don't care." Ague shook her head fiercely, causing dried leaves to fly from the webbing of her hair.

"Hush now. Where is your paisley?"

"I threw it away. I hate it. I hate you. I like you better in the dreams. When we are fairies!"

"Hate not, Ague."

"Leaf."

"*Ague*. We have been through this."

"Why can't I go into Papa's room?"

"Why would you want to?"

"To see the ghost."

"Why don't you go outside and look for your paisley. You shouldn't hurt your sister by throwing away a present."

Ague needed little persuasion and was ushered from her little chair to the door. Hemlocke took her place by the fireplace and proceeded to busy herself with her embroidery. She did not notice her sister had stopped in the doorway and stared at her with a menacing expression that could chill the blood of the most daring.

"I saw Rusalka[29] again…."

"You did not."

"With Papa. Papa is dead."

"Ague. Enough," here Hemlocke threw her knitting into her lap before calming herself; "Still your troubled heart, feeble sister."

The violent deadpan that had arrested Ague's face faded instantly, returning to bright-eyed naivety. She threw the door shut behind her, leaving her sister alone with the silence.

The few seconds that followed this uncouth egress sent a shudder down Hemlocke's spine. Breath escaped her in a sharp and fearful staccato, for the silence was suddenly so

---

[29] *Rusalka:* Water woman of Slavic folklore. Said to be the souls of women drowned. Some iterations of Rusalka appear as will-o-the-wisps; children born out of wedlock and drowned by their mothers.

encompassing as to render her feeling helplessly vulnerable. It would not take her long to resolutely shake such ridiculous thoughts, reminding herself that this was in fact her home, her domain, and that which had rattled her so was merely the behaviour of her immature sister.

Thorn. Why did her sister incessantly name her thus? The esoteric argot employed by her twin frustrated the more equable Hemlocke; she felt the agnomen bestowed upon her by Ague a great injustice to her constitution. Did her sister really think her so cold? The loveless imagery evoked by such a harsh title led Hem to doubt the capacity of her matriarchal ability. It was the absence of their tragically perished mother that had Hemlocke assuming a certain level of maternal duty - be it wilfully assigned or not - and to have Ague treat her with such childish disdain cut her heart deeply. It had been a long time since she had felt happiness, so long that she had begun to doubt she ever felt it at all. Perhaps it had not been happiness, rather a denial of what she had been forced to become; in that sense, she was very much like her daydreaming sister. She could not blame Ague. After all, when had they ever been allowed to be little girls? Thrust into responsibility that no child should endure so young, Hemlocke had shiftlessly abided to her father's expectations, while Ague had lurched so far into the abyss of madness that there was no recovering her sanity.

The vermillion glow of the fire offered warmth to her overworked mind, yet even in that nurturing nest before it, employed with her embroidery Hem could not shut out the tenebrific thoughts that plagued her; thoughts that dwelled on the past, palpitated through the present and feared for the future. She carried stoicism in her composure, but it was her lack of trust in others that held her back from truly relinquishing any small amount of control. Were anyone to ever meet her pedantic standards she may have been able to do so, and by result experience a fulfilled relief deserving of one as overworked as she.

Now that their father, the once venerable Walpole Wight, was decamped as it were, it fell to Hem once again to reign in her sister's flippancy, keeping her own head above water all the while. Presently she sighed, as though such a mechanical action could relieve the fact that she knew too much, withheld too much, and possessed inadequate sources with which to share her burden. The fire crackled indifferently in the hearth.

With the wind moaning through the stairwell, the estate creaked in its joints and shivered on its foundations. The trees, once sturdy in their stance now hurled their branches southbound; pressured by the north wind they pointed, as though they could escape to a warmer clime were they to reach far enough. But their cruel roots held the trunks fast while the gale lashed viciously and stripped the leafy coats from the boughs. There amongst them, a late summer leaf on the breeze, Ague spun. She was a dryad. She *was* Leaf. In her mind the forest was hers; the wind was the voice of a nurturing friend. It was here that she felt her mother's presence with unshakable force, despite her perishing when Leaf was only a newborn, and as such the poor girl never shook away the idea that she was a child of the forest.

Having been so affected by her sister's words moments earlier, it would have appeared unusual to see Leaf in such high spirits. Indeed the evidence of her melancholy showed shamelessly in the dried crust of tears that hardened in the wind, but her countenance bore a mysterious smile - a smile both blithe and content. She stopped spinning for a moment and closed her eyes, allowing the wind to rush around her. The village lay some distance down the road, though its structures could not be seen from her vantage point, and she believed herself to be one more tree in the sea of green that was her world. She wore her goose-bumped flesh like bark, the blood of her veins running like cold sap, and like every other tree in the forest she watched. Her eyes scanned the ground with a hawk-like precision, until something foreign, something that didn't belong in the scene, caught her gaze. Racing towards the disturbance she smirked, pleased with her ability to find her precious paisley, which glared green and summery from the autumnal foliage that nestled it. Leaf procured a shoe string from her boot with the intent of slipping the amulet onto it as a makeshift necklace, but instead she coiled the lace tightly around her wrist and gritted her teeth fiercely. The cord that bound her to her sister had given up slack as Thorn matured, and Leaf threw the frustration of her loneliness against that cord, vainly trying to rope her sister back to a time when they were both childish and to an extent, carefree. The necklace slipped back around her collar, the cold stone of malachite[30] chilled her, even through her clothing, and she shuddered on recollection of her isolation. For a moment, the veil had been lifted, exposing her inadequate joviality for the gauche charlatan that it was, so that she stood on the verge of desperate sobs that would remain unheard by the wind. The nature she had claimed as matriarch had abandoned her; she shivered involuntarily and suddenly broke into a run through the trees.

When she had reached a clearing of sorts, the trunks gave way to the ramshackle buildings of her crude village. Decay drifted on the wind's breath, carrying with it the debris of arcane lives; glass bottles, old rags, ashes - these were but a few of the remnants locked in time by the people who had long since abandoned the town. An old water wheel spun in the greasy canal, not through human exertion but rather those ghostly winds, so that the poisonous scum that stained the waterways churned agonisingly. Leaf walked the streets with confidence unbroken, for it was this abandoned village that had become her domain; considering Thorn rarely ventured

---

[30] *Malachite:* Green ore mined in the Urals.

beyond the estate grounds, and the hermitage kept by her late father, Leaf alone claimed the wreckage. She knew the alleys by memory, the environs altered solely by the steady disintegration of nature, so it was only proper that her tranquillity would come undone upon the intrusive noise of a horse's whinny. Her heart lurched. Creeping cautiously onto the main thoroughfare she spied a caravan parked where there was not supposed to be anything at all. Leaf looked around and, seeing no other living creature but those horses, wandered slowly towards them. The caravan was colourful; a garish sight for the drab background on which it lay. A twist of rage contorted Leaf's psyche, and she kicked the wheel of the caravan with aggression. The caravan did not budge, and the pain that shot through her ankle made Leaf wince. She had to get away from that wretched eyesore; somewhere she could once again breathe deep the scents of the forest.

Further beyond the town the trees regathered and pressed closer together until the terrain became almost impossible to traverse. Yet Leaf continued her mission, accepting the challenge that nature's obstacle course offered her. Scrambling over fallen trunks, across moss-cloaked boulders and lichen-choked roots she began a steady descent down a steep slope to where the icy lake waited for her below. The sun had begun to set, the ethereal light that it cast through the cloud cover painted the scene with flashes of bright colour - the wisps appeared in their hundreds. Floating gently above the lake waters they beckoned Leaf, whose heart leapt with joy at their sight, for she saw the ghost lights as the eyes of her mother watching her. Although the lake was covered by a sheet of ice she found a small black patch at the water's edge where the ice had broken away in slabs, the water beneath thick and sluggish with fatigue. Removing her necklace, Leaf proceeded to dangle the paisley over the water surface so that the reflection swung like an inverted pendulum. She fancied that she could see the haunting face of her mother staring blue and wide-eyed up at her, hair swaying in the current like seaweed. Leaf reached forth her hand slowly, but when her fingertip met the icy water she flinched and the vision was lost all at once. The clouds above, swollen with snow began to spit their flakes earthbound, their frigid petals blurring the surface of the lake so that Leaf could no longer see below it.

The girl sighed and sat back on her haunches, allowing her gaze to drift aimlessly toward the other side of the lake. The ghost lights stared back, their luminous orbs not unlike fireflies on a night much warmer than the one promised to her. But there was a peculiar pair of lights that arrested her sight. A trance held her, and she might have fancied that she looked upon her own reflection. There, staring back at her from across the lake, stood a man.

X : At Wight Estate

"Whoso rewardeth evil for good, evil shall not depart from his house."
-      Proverbs 17:13 (KJV)

In the old drawing room atop the airy atrium of Wight
Estate, the fire burned with a new vigour. The heat it gave
off kept the house itself from feeling completely dead as a
triad of strange figures huddled around it to warm
themselves. Outside the wind howled with the cries of the
early evening; it reminded the inhabitants of its
omnipotence, that their little fire could only warm them
for so long. The room itself was moth-eaten; the acrid
scent of mildew seeped from the floorboards, coiling its
odours about the dust-clumped furniture and adding to the
loveless sepia hue of its walls. One of these inhabitants,
the man known only as Viy, sat mollified and unabashed
upon a luxurious armchair, where he crossed his crisp legs
and gently puffed at his cigarette. He showed no interest
or even notice to the exchange undertaken by his two
companions, one of them being none other than Mr.
Pinnacle Tricks. The awkward young man scratched at his
bird-mad hair and tapped his feet impatiently among other
involuntary twitches, for his unease had been amplified by
the young woman sitting across from him who refused to
cease staring at him. This woman, whom we recognise to
be Ague Wight, did not stare at her visitor with malice,
rather her curiosity led her to remain fixated in her gaze;
her empty smile coinciding with this stare could easily have
been portrayed as intimidating. The prospect of a visitor
was one so foreign to the girl that it pressed the limits of
her faltered social skills. Tricks looked to Viy for some
assistance but, finding none, tried desperately to dispel the

tension that only he had sense to notice.

"You are Wight's daughter?"

"You mean Papa? Papa is dead. Am I still his daughter?"

Tricks coughed, "I'm terribly sorry. I did not mean to offend. You have my commiserations."

"What's that?"

He felt he could howl in anguish, "I, er, never mind. Is your sister…?"

Ague followed Pinnacle's pointed finger to the door, "She is making us food. Are you a dryad[31]?"

"Beg pardon?"

"A dryad. I found you by the lake. You must be a dryad."

"I… I don't understand you," he turned to his companion, "I say, Viy…?"

"Hmm?" Viy turned his head lazily from the fire but offered nothing further to the strange conversation.

"Well I am a dryad," continued Ague, "My name is Leaf."

"Your name is Ague." here Hemlocke entered the room with a tray of breads and coffee.

"Horrible Thorn." replied her sister.

Hemlocke placed the tray down amongst the company and brushed her hands over her smock. She then took it upon herself to stoke the fire, and as she stooped over the fireplace her dark curls swung slowly as though they were an extension of the flames, intermingling with the soft billows of smoke that drifted upwards from them. Unbeknownst to the triad behind her, Hemlocke's heart pounded furiously. She was not inclined to company at the best of times, and prayed that her flummoxed disposition was not betrayed by any quivering of knees or stuttering of words. She had to remain sturdy during this transaction, as per the wishes of her father. Presently she turned, her

---

[31] *Dryad:* A forest nymph.

form haloed by the fire behind her like some celestial eclipse.

"I understand that you must have expected a more decent reception, sirs," she said, "Had I known the exactness of your arrival we could have welcomed you more conventionally."

"Think nothing of it, Miss," replied Tricks, "a little fright or fear of ghosts is entirely my imagination's fault, to be sure!"

"He saw the ghost, too." Ague whispered.

Hemlocke shot her a glare, "Ague! We have company - this is no time for your silly fantasies!"

The emaciated twin appeared to ignore her sister's scolding, instead reaffirming the unsettling stare she had fixated upon Pinnacle Tricks. Pinnacle found himself shivering involuntarily at the girl's remark.

"Unfortunately, nobody lives in the village anymore." continued Hemlocke.

"None? You live alone out here?" said Tricks.

Hemlocke nodded and stoked the fire again, "Some cited a poisoned water supply, but that is just frivolous folklore. Really the villagers petered out slowly over the years - Father would have attested to this. And could I hold blame on any of them? Who would want to live in this miserable corner of the world?"

"There is an ethereal beauty in these latitudes." piped Viy.

"You do not need to flatter us. My sister and I know nothing else. We have lived here since birth; were it not for my picture books and my father's knowledge, well, I would think the pines to be the very edge of the world."

Pinnacle insisted she sit down, taking the coffee pot from her grasp and filling the cups himself.

There is strength in this woman, he thought, believing without doubt that her strange frailty was the result of grief. Ague on the other hand was clearly inhibited, perhaps she was clouding herself from the family tragedy, or perhaps that was just how she was.

"I must comment on your remarkable English." said Tricks.

"Hmm? Well Father was British after all," replied Hemlocke. "He was able to converse with the villagers in their tongue but always spoke his native language when at home."

"A fine skill," winked Viy.

Of course, thought Tricks, *how else would he have known Fairlie?*

"Nothing grows here," said Hemlocke, "the snow chokes all but the pines; it is remarkable that the village prospered as long as it did. But father was a reclusive man. He essentially formed the village himself - the people all worked for him. I think he must have wanted his own world contained, barren though it may have ended up; such was his desire to be alone that he would choose to persevere with a harsh life."

Pinnacle was reminded of his superior, Mr. Fairlie. This Mr. Wight seemed to have been a miser of similar standards, but he didn't dare express such a thought to the grieving girls.

"Almost like a castle of old," said Tricks, "with the commons at the feet of the affluent, surrounding the walls."

"Quite." said Viy.

"He did not like England?" asked Tricks.

Hemlocke frowned, "Honestly, he rarely mentioned it. But I am sure you know more about his days in Britain than I would, Mr. Fairlie."

Silence fell sharply among them. Pinnacle felt his heart sink to hear her words and struggled to articulate his thoughts and clear the confusion. He could not help but feel that he was intruding on a clandestine business; that he was a meddling in affairs that seethed at his presence. Looking at Hemlocke sitting across from him, her perpetual frown seemed to intensify with the confusion;

Tricks imagined the feminine spectre he had espied in the village standing at his host's shoulder. That sickening feeling of terror he had felt on those desolate streets returned; at that moment she - *it* - felt truly tangible, as though that icy face was that of a fifth inhabitant to the room. The wind seemed to howl in his ears, and Tricks turned desperately toward Viy for assistance again.

"Is there a problem?" asked Hemlocke softly.

"I... I am not Mr. Fairlie," said Tricks.

Hemlocke struggled to comprehend the issue and, turning to Viy, said, "Oh! I am so sorry. *You* are Mr. Fairlie?"

Viy shook his head indifferently as Hemlocke grew as pale as her sister, "Neither of you is Ereven Fairlie?"

"I am his assistant," said Pinnacle Tricks, "I have been sent in his stead. This man here is my translator and guide."

"Fairlie is not here," repeated Hemlocke, as if to clarify to herself.

"Not here! Not here!" giggled Ague, who was brutishly dunking bread into her coffee cup.

While Ague remained twitterpated with the lunacy plaguing her brain, the sounder members of the room gaped for comprehension of the issue that had arisen. Feeling very much the nomad, Pinnacle Tricks hoped that his presence in lieu of Fairlie would not present itself as an insurmountable obstacle for the completion of his task. Little did he know that Hemlocke struggled with similar thoughts; she had been prepared for Ereven Fairlie to arrive at their home. What protocol was she to follow in his absence? The Sisyphean nature of her toil was all too much to burden, and she cursed the tears threatening to spill from her dark eyes.

She restrained herself, simply stating, "There appears to be a problem."

"Please, the blame falls to us," said Tricks, "you should have been made aware the notion to have me resolve this in my master's stead. Fool all the more that I assumed Mr. Fairlie to have informed you."

"This is fine," Hemlocke stuttered, and then as if to reassure herself, "this is fine."

Neither party appear to know where to tread from that moment. Hemlocke resolutely steeled herself; this was just another problem she had to address herself. Her mind stung with an anxiety that clouded any clear thoughts of progression. For the sake of her father, she needed time to work out her next step.

"I hate to sound forceful during what must be a difficult time for you, but I was sent to collect the deeds of that which was left to my master."

"I understand," replied Hemlocke, "it is what father told me to do. I am confused though, as he wished *very specifically* for me to hand over to Mr. Fairlie himself..."

Tricks shrugged slowly, lost for any response.

"Well," she continued, "it is late, and you've little choice but to stay the night. We can resolve matters tomorrow."

"Very kind of you." replied Tricks purely out of etiquette, although he sighed inwardly to realise he was delayed once again. He longed to return home and be done with the whole ordeal. Across the room, Ague continued to stare at her visitors, that same expression pasted on her face - unsettling and vacant. Pinnacle gritted his teeth and suppressed a frustrated groan. Hemlocke too, felt stress lay heavily on her heart, but the coming of night meant she had hours to collect herself and figure out her course of action. As they all stood to egress, Ague's smile grew slowly maniacal, until she could contain herself no longer and said, "You saw her too..."

Pinnacle Tricks felt a chill creep down his spine; he turned to where Ague was seated, "Pardon?"

"Blue..." whispered Ague teasingly, "Blue but with red eyes... Even at the lake bottom the eyes burn..."

"That's enough, Ague!" snapped Hemlocke.

"It's Leaf!"

A revelation dawned on Pinnacle Tricks. *Leaf.* Where had he heard that before? *The will!* The witness who had signed with such childish penmanship - was this the girl? Surely it had to be, but to have signed such an important document with a pseudonym? Something didn't sit right; there was a nagging at the back of Pinnacle's mind that he could not pinpoint. Then it hit him - yes, he clearly recalled the words of Mr. Dergatsya - that of Wight having had *no known family.* Now before him were two young women claiming to be the man's daughters. Surely logic said that Wight's immediate kin would inherit the bulk of his estate. But why would his own daughter, this *Leaf,* sign away her fortunes to Mr. Fairlie, who for all he knew could have been completely unknown to the girls. Why would Hemlocke, who was clearly the more sound of the two, have not signed in her stead? Furthermore, where were these girls to live? Unease crept deviously into Pinnacle's heart, and Leaf's mentioning of ghostly spectres did little to harden his resolve. But there his musing would be postponed, as Hemlocke, almost as though she wished to distract him, ushered her two guests to their quarters.

XI : The Journal of Pinnacle Tricks

"In the pines, where the sun never shines, I shivered the whole night through."

-    Unknown[32]

I had transcribed my conversation with Wight's daughters in the form of a few important points that I won't mention again. Let Fairlie deal with it, should he ever receive my letter. The two young ladies both have a mystic quality to them that makes me feel quite uneasy; this is no doubt a quality of having been left in isolation for so long. I think it cruel that their father would seclude them from the outside world so, but then again I am not a father myself yet, so my opinion is of little value. However, I could not help but feel an intruder in this place, as to why, well that was obvious. I had not been expected, and by extension had not been welcome. Perhaps it was that they had expected Mr. Fairlie as a fatherly shoulder to lean in such a dire time - having been robbed of their patriarch, I can seldom blame them.

Viy sleeps soundly across the room. The man frustrates me somewhat; there is a cheery optimism to him that is indisputably misleading. This should not be a trait that robs me of confidence, but alas it does. For who can trust the man who is always happy? Solomon tells of the 'days of darkness[33]', and how there 'will be many of them'; I can't help but feel that Viy hides behind a fabricated

---

[32] *Unknown:* A lyric from a traditional American folk song, sometimes titled *In the pines* or *Black girl.*

[33] *Days of darkness:* Ecclesiastes 11:8. King Solomon is often thought to have been the author.

ignorance, although I suppose it is an ignorance I could envy.

The guest rooms here at Wight Estate are well-furnished despite their obvious disuse. The years of neglect had left freshly made beds frozen in time and enveloped with dust, but remained a far cry from the uncomfortable journey in the caravan from Petersburg. The comfort of this fire lifts my spirits, as does the fine coffee Viy had brewed for me before retiring to sleep. Upon my request for him to partake of coffee with me he respectfully declined, citing an anxiety for insomnia as reason. Perhaps he had a good point there, but I do not wish to sleep myself. Were I to try, I believe I would only fail; questions are begging for answers, and loose ends lay tangled - awaiting to be tied.

Our converse this afternoon has left me in disarray; I remain unsure of my next objective and it seemed that Miss Hemlocke is as confused as me. I have written to Mr. Fairlie, but I have doubts that he will receive my letter in time, as Hemlocke informed me that the post arrives but once a week. I shudder at the thought of remaining here, but in my desperation I realise that this may be my lot until I hear of my next order. Trapped! Pinned by slow post and opaque orders! Confound this clandestine mission of Fairlie. The man cares little for my own well-being. Would that I could quit my post and work elsewhere, but such a move would not bode well for my wife and I. I have written to Edythe, though now I feel foolish to have expunged such a lugubrious dribble. Pitiful man to moan as I do. I wrote as one does in love's florid infancy when the reality is our marriage is aged and sturdy. 'Old souls' - that was how my mother described it, although that would be mostly attribute to Edythe, for she is wise beyond her years. Yet I continue to want the best for her, naive though I can be, and if that means my being absent for a touch longer, so be it. Wracked with a writhing of suspended hope I must wait.

****

I return to my journal now in the early hours of the dawn. I know not what time it is; however - the sun will not rise for some time yet - this blasted winter delays the day to a criminal extent. This house echoes with the mutterings of wind and snow, but this surely cannot account for the noises in which I've recently heard. My palms sweat as I pen this, yet I am wracked with shivers - this room has lost all warmth to the night's cruel grasp. There had been a brief feeling of reprieve when I had retired to sleep; I felt at last the embrace of comfortable slumber for a moment. Old though this house may be, its lodgings burdened the load I had carried for days on end, and I was grateful to slumber in a warm bed with the winter kept at bay by sturdy walls. My mind wandered with a fluttering symphony of light and sound, of shadows flickering behind candlelight and the distant gales wailing through a maze of pine and moonlight. This daze slipped me from consciousness and into that nostalgic realm of dreams, where the familiar image of my wife rose before me. I often dream of her, and tonight it was unchanged - once more I found myself chasing her, and in spite of my cries to wait for me she simply laughed and ran, taunting me to hurry along behind her. A sound thundered with every footfall, a thumping of hearts and the murmur of blood flowing. I fancied I detected voices around me, though I could not locate their whereabouts. At this point I felt myself drawn slowly toward awakening, for the crimson contours of the ceiling above my bed came into view, my eyes lazily tracing imaginary patterns with childish naivety. The metronomic thump continued, and my ears filled with the faint sounds of chanting. It was a sound both haunting and primal, like that of monastery or some tribe of land afar. For a long time I lay there, merely ignoring the noise and dismissing it as a figment of imagination. On a sudden

my eyes were properly opened, and there was no doubt of
my being awake. Still that noctambulous rondo[34]
continued, my mind trying to comprehend its origin like
one who misses the first part of a story. Could Viy be
snoring? I cast my gaze to where he lay heavily in his bed.
No - that chanting was not one of snores. Viy's form rose
and fell to the different rhythm of his own breathing.
Surely, thought I, my head is just aching with the release of
tension built over the days of travel. Curling over in the
bed I tried to ignore the dirge that grew steadily in volume.
It soon became impossible to ignore, thundering in my
ears with an urgent intensity. I rose.

Opening the door, the corridor sent a sickly creep of
cold into the room, the hall so dark and clammy I half
expected to see ice growing on the walls. The chanting was
louder in the hallway; I strained my hearing to locate its
source. Despite its all-encompassing drone, I was able to
focus on a single point of origin, and readily began to
move along the corridor towards it. The voices were
unintelligible; maybe they were of some ancient and
perished language, but I could not discern any Latin quality
to it. There had to be a logical answer. Did Wight Estate
have some small church hall? Were there villagers
worshipping at some sort of midnight mass? Although the
idea carried more logic than a fear of ghosts, it sounded
absurd - Hemlocke had already confirmed the village to be
empty of residents.

The corridors carried on, seemingly endless in their
twists and turns. Some sconces cradled weakening candles,
casting a dull glow of light before the corridor plunged
into darkness again. It reminded me of streetlamps on a
dark road, coming and passing with my approach.
Entranced, I rounded the corner again and froze to a

---

[34] *Rondo:* A musical movement where a principle theme is
repeated at least three times in response to two or more
contrasting themes.

standstill. The phantom - that dark figure I had seen in the village - for but an instant appeared at the far end of the corridor. My heart lurched; the figure didn't seem to notice me, and was visible for only the slightest moment as it strode slowly along a corridor perpendicular to the where I stood. My knees shook, and that maddening chant bellowed louder than before. Above the melodic din I heard the distinct sound of a door opening and closing; the figure I had seen had entered some room at the end of the corridor. The din briefly escalated to an ear-aching pitch, before becoming muffled once more; whatever the source of that noise may have been was behind the door just breached by my eldritch stalker. I felt damp with cold sweat - that sickly dread that reminds one of an awful bout of influenza. Had I the courage to further my quest towards that door? The closer I crept, the chanting enveloped me, once again I thought of ancient monasteries; the door at the corridor's end was rattling on its hinges. Accompanying the rhythmic drone of chanting was the horrible percussion of banging upon the door - something was apparently beating against it from the other side. My heart raced faster, floating towards my throat with fear, but my resolve had not failed me yet. Through some mechanical motion I reached for the doorknob when - to my horror - the sounds, the banging, the chanting, all of it stopped, and a silence so deafening cut through the air. I felt my breath come sharply, catching in my throat before shivering into a petrified exhale.

The door, featureless, mahogany, stood sentinel-still before me. The onslaught of quiet struck me harder than I would have expected, and the thrumming of my threadbare heart pounding in my chest made me curse. For now it was too quiet, and my breath broke the silence intensely. A whisper of voices entered my ears - how long had I remained standing paralysed? The voices were no longer that of chants but rather the familiar sounds of a tête-à-tête[35]. One of them was undoubtedly Hemlocke, and

I envisaged that she must be rather close to the door, as her voice came easily to me. She was obviously in converse with an inaudible party; one that I could not discern to be male or female for the volume of their speech was much too soft. Again I felt myself to be an intruder; my eavesdropping aside, I thought I caught Hemlocke's voice mentioning 'Fairlie', 'the estate', before the more sinister phrase - 'he must be dealt with accordingly'.

Feeling the shivers of fear creep over me once more I turned to return to my room; I did not belong here, I was dabbling in matters of which I was an unwelcome intruder. The corridor from whence I'd come was dimly lit by candlelight, the nightly shadows tricking my eyes to envisaging a horrible banshee[36] hovering outside a nearby window. Her hair lay in shambles over her face as blood-dipped nails scraped menacingly at the pane. Stricken, I hit the floor running, propelled by a hideous shriek that echoed from behind me. I had to be imagining things! Foolishly, I turned in my panicked run and fancied that the banshee followed in toe, her eyes alive with fire and hatred. My lungs burned with this fearful fire, I did not stop until I made it to this room, after which the relief that washed over me was indescribable. All at once the silence returned, and when I was finally able to calm the rabbit thump of my heart I could hear nothing but Viy's gentle snoring. The wind continued its southbound journey, the candle flickered weakly, and I was without doubt alone in my awakened state.

Until now I had not thought of myself as superstitious, but I am unable to account for the things I experienced tonight - the noctambulous rondo, that mysterious conversation, *that horrible spectre...* I lay in bed, shivering

---

[35] *Tête-à-tête:* French. A private conversation between two people; also *vis-à-vis.*

[36] *Banshee:* Of Irish folklore – a female ghost whose wailing is often interpreted as a premonition of forthcoming death.

with an awful cold sweat and prayed that this was all mere fever dream, prayed that sleep would return to me soon, but the hour of dawn is on its way. My mind won't rest - not tonight - and although I have claimed to be sceptical of ghosts and ghouls, I feel the need to pen what I've seen since arriving at this forsaken locale. I want to go home.

XII : Atlas Egerton
London, 1888

"Nothing thicker than a knife's blade separates happiness from melancholy."

- Virginia Woolf

The London boulevardes had quietened as the night wore on, and when Big Ben struck its sombre tones and ushered in the midnight birth of a new day there were but few carriages left trundling over the bridges of the Thames. Within one of those stately mansions that lined the river near Waterloo, a gentleman sat by his fireplace watching the fractured copper light of the fire shining through his tumbler. Ereven Fairlie, of aquiline grace, mused in melancholic dignity. Though slouched somewhat in his recumbent state the man exuded an air of dominance, a barrier that hid his true despondency; despondency for a woman he had once loved, a woman who had once lived and now lived no more. Even while he swirled the swiftly diminishing drink another figure cut from dejection pottered around in cobweb-choked shadows of the mansion. It was Atlas Egerton - faithful servant of Ereven Fairlie - noble conduct dripping from his moustache, in spite of aching knee joints, of gloom-crippled heart and mind. He had followed the unchanging train of his tasks; freshened bed sheets, dusted mantles and now entered the drawing room with the day's mail clasped in his gloved hands. He held the letters away from his person as though they were a dreadful thing to be rid of, and approached his master with the same respect he had shown for years.

"Word from Master Pinnacle, sir."

"Tricks, is it? So the young man made it to Russia,

eh what?"

"I had my reservations as to whether he would make it."

The chuckle that escaped Ereven Fairlie was cracked and brittle, sounded perhaps more sinister than intended; a quality attributed in part to his humourless demeanour.

"Well go ahead then, read it."

Atlas cleared his throat, "Care of Wight Estate Finland -"

Fairlie started, the words had struck a blow at his heart and Atlas paused hesitantly in his dictation.

"Shall I continue, sir?"

"*Wight Estate*? The boy is *at* Wight Estate?"

"I-I am merely a messenger, sir." replied Atlas.

"Best leave them here, good man."

Atlas placed the letters on the table and refreshed his master's drink only to be waved away. He stared expectantly at the ensconced man; Fairlie grasped the letter to confirm the postmark with his own eyes, before gazing thoughtfully into the hearth. He had expected to hear from Pinnacle once he reached Saint Petersburg, never did he imagine the boy to make the trip into the endless forests of Lapland. For a moment the pair were statue still, and if not for the flickering shadows cast by the flames they could have been the subjects of a painting captured forever in autumnal brushstrokes. In time Fairlie seemed to remember the presence of his servant and, desiring the fruits of isolation, thought to dismiss the man.

"You may retire, Egerton," he said, "that will be all this evening."

His voice had grown strangely weak; the manservant noticed as such but would not dare to mention it.

"Sir."

Bowing with panache, Atlas Egerton left his master to his musing.

The echoes of footsteps rhythmically interrupted the weary silence that draped itself in cold fronds over the manor. The footsteps were those of Atlas Egerton; the man having been relieved of his duties now crossed the marble tiles and begun the ascent towards his quarters. His hands clasped pensively behind his back, Atlas took each sombre step as a sharp blow to his stony countenance; each step chipped a small piece away, and he prayed he could reach his room before the illusion of composure was broken. His pace grew swifter; the tapping unsettling him further like a clock ticking down towards impending self-destruction. Any joy he may have had in his possession slowly seeped from him, lost to the cloying misery of the night, until he enclosed himself in his room and the only metronomic sound that remained was the dusky thrum of his heartbeat. An insatiable gloom overcame him. Perhaps it was because he was in his late fifties and he had begun to feel the afternoon sunlight shine sadly on his shoulders. It could have been that he realised he could never be twenty again, sipping coffee in a Barcelona bar, thinking of the flowers yet to be brought to bloom by life's fleeting kiss. Maybe it was because his wife had been gone for five years now and each day only worsened the deep cut that was left in his heart. The shivering frailty that came with aged grief soon thickened in Atlas' throat until the back of his neck cramped and his teeth grit. He could not bring his youth back, could not bring his wife back; yet he knew he had to rein in some control over his life before he drifted further from the pier of harmony. Atlas shuffled to his writing desk and prepared a fresh pot of ink. In his advanced age he had little to keep him occupied, but his opus-in-making - a lengthy poem titled *'Gull & Leviathan'* - gave him some inkling towards a goal achieved, small as it may have appeared. Atlas had tinkered with the work for years, as though he were afraid to ever call it finished; the concept had floated in his mind for that long, but it had only been recently that he had joined words together into something tangible. At that moment he wondered whether it was the right time to be writing. He was paralysed by his depression and knew that it would be an uphill battle to produce anything worthwhile, yet how else could he vent the mounting pressure in his soul?

The pen quivered in his grasp. The first mark of ink left on his page would not be anything eloquent; rather his hesitation led to a drop of ink perspiring from the pen and staining the crisp parchment. This blemishing of his canvas seemed to kick his mind into motion, and like an old clock that groans awake with the crunch of new gears turning, he scribbled a few words down:

Spake again, Leviathan, "Why comest thou to thee?"

Atlas paused. The melody was good. He allowed the metre to wash over him, swaying melodically as he mumbled the words under his breath.

Spake again, Leviathan, "Why comest thou to thee?"

All at once an air of doubt exhumed its vapours from the poet's brain, and Atlas bethought himself to have committed a terminal faux pas[37]. The error glared at him, and as an artist who cannot help but dwell on the most miniscule brushstroke otherwise unnoticed by the observer Atlas clasped his head in frustration. *Thou to thee* - did that line make sense? No. *Thou to me* would be more appropriate - but to think of the polish lost upon the removal of alliteration! He was torn. Eventually the urge to follow correct grammar overtook and with a decisive stroke of the pen Atlas drew a line through his artistic want. Again he pondered the choice he had made; siding once more with what society deemed 'fit'. The melody of his verse which had previously lulled him to reverie had soured, leaving him with little choice but to slam his notebook shut. His temple throbbed; his throat hot and tense with emotive bursts of passion, torture and dissatisfaction - all of which attempted to purge

---

[37] *Faux pas:* French – literally 'false step'.

themselves from him, only to become choked in his chest.

The nocturnal gusts continued to howl into his open casement, growling past the voice box window frame with indifferent purpose; his candle guttered out instantly, and any comforting light surrounding Atlas vanished into the muted moonlight. Cursing, he fumbled with a book of matches; his functions refusing to cooperate with one another, failing eyes squinting weakly and fingers shivering. The casement was slammed shut, the candle re-lit, and Atlas flinched as his fingertips were burnt by the dwindling match stick. The shock of this small burn drew him further away from his artistic purpose and he knew fully well that he could write no more tonight.

Atlas heaved a heavy sigh that could easily have tumbled into a sob. Surely he would cry if he wished it, but to what purpose? Was anything truly wrong? He closed his eyes for a moment as if to test whether he would be allowed a reprieve of tears to wash clean some of the darkness that cloaked him. But the years of melancholia had left him as little more than a husk of a man; the brittleness that came with fresh despondency had long since hardened into mere repression. He knew the beast well; knew the stickiness of its webs, clinging stubbornly to his person, with the residue of its effects lingering long after he had thought himself beyond a current episode of gloom.

I refuse to be ordinary.

Although it may have been his battle cry, his actions did little to reflect his conviction. The protagonists of his opus *'Gull & Leviathan'* reflected the conflicting natures at war for his attention. The gull - rash, naive, though the mark of the Machiavellian branded his feathers. The leviathan - possessing of wisdom beyond the length of the chains that anchored him to his island home. At least that was what he intended for his characters, were he to ever finish the work.

I refuse to be ordinary.

Yet there he sat, a tatterdemalion ripped and ragged from the inside out. His drive, once a steadfast bronco, had dug its heels into the sand until the resistance gave way and buckled to convention. Atlas' thoughts turned to Pinnacle Tricks. Yes, he knew the lad. Credulous boy, but given his age it was surely to no fault of his own. The weight of world had not had time to settle on the boy's narrow shoulders[38]. Yet there he was, immersed in the spirit of the vagabond; travelling, wandering from one place to another with art and the north wind for company. Meanwhile Atlas remained a hesitant hermit in his humble home. Home though it may be, it had grown stagnant with each taunt of the adventurous renegade that whispered so frequently in his ear. What was it that chained his heart to normalcy? In his fancy Atlas would have insisted on going in Pinnacle's stead, but such actions would have indeed been a crass dream. For he was but an ordinary servant, and as such etiquette forbade it.

Suum cuique[39].

As a wave that crashes shore-bound and struggles to detach itself from the amorphous mass that is its root, its life pulse, so too did Atlas wrestle to be rid of his anxiety. If only he could command convention to go its own way, whereby he would follow his in the opposite direction. But it was those conventions that kept him in work, kept him drawing income, kept him alive. Why was man so helpless against the tide? Why must his efforts to crest the wave summit be repaid with an indifferent drifting?
Why could a man not be fulfilled by his thoughts, paid by his joy, enriched by dreams that became plans that became reality? Fear had led him to where he was, and it was doubt

---

[38] *The weight of the world... shoulders:* In Greek mythology, Atlas was the name of a titan condemned by Zeus to burden the world (Gaia) on his shoulders for all eternity.
[39] *Suum cuique:* Latin – literally 'to each his own'.

that held him from where he wanted to be.

I refuse to be ordinary.

Would that be the refrain that carried him into sleep? He lay himself down on the stiff mattress, bothering not to don his nightclothes and merely kicking his shoes to the floor. A moment later he would be up again, agonised by the lack of symmetry in his discarded shoes, placing them neatly by the foot of the bed. Surely his depression had peaked; he had plummeted down sin's slippery slope into a pit of self-loathing, inasmuch as he lay face down into his pillow and muttered in syllables discernible only to himself.

I am completely tormented.

XIII : Correspondents

"Nothing will come of nothing. Speak again."

-       William Shakespeare

From the pen of Pinnacle Tricks;

Ereven,

My greetings to you from the East. I pray the London
weather has held out sunny for you as it was when I left.
My journey has been an eventful one, and I fear that
perhaps I have been set on a misguided course - a 'wild
goose chase' as it were. I write to you from the Wight
Estate in Lapland, where I have been flushed to after my
original destination of Saint Petersburg. I had agreed to my
task being one simply of messenger, as you had informed
me, good sir. Surely you must have had some hint about
this - my being sent miles away from course? Naught
seems organised; Wight's lawyer - this Dergatsya - has
been of little assistance and would appear to know less of
the situation than I do. And since Wight himself cannot
clear matters up for me (Lord rest his soul), it has fallen to
his young daughters to resolve. As misfortune would have
it, they too have little idea on my purpose in being here,
and I refrain from pressing business matters upon people
who are mourning. So to you sir, the facts - Wight has left
his estate to you, this much I know, but I fear the title
cannot be passed through me, a messenger. You see I am
at a loss; having experienced some trying times (some I
wish not to expand upon in written correspondence), I
must please ask of you the permission to return home and
resume my regular life and duties. The confusion regarding
the will is one that is beyond my abilities, and one that you
(with utmost respect), must resolve yourself, sir. I await

your direction in regards to my next move and pray you will take my requests on board. Please let Edythe know that I am missing her terribly.

With regards,

Pinnacle Tricks.

From the pen of Ereven Fairlie;

Tricks,

I admire you to have managed so far from home. Forgive the tardiness of this response; I am sure you are seeing firsthand the isolation in which old Wight absorbed himself; am certain the post will be slow. I am not impressed with the situation as it stands. I left for you the specific order of collecting whatever may be left to me in the will; I cannot allow you to return until those matters are resolved. You know I am a busy man and have my own matters to attend to; therefore it will be up to you to figure out what to do. As my astute young protégé, I have faith that you are up to the task. I understand your homesickness but you must see out the job assigned to you. Home will be here when you return.

Regards,

Fairlie.

From the pen of Pinnacle Tricks;

My love,

I write to you from a distance that would shock you. This assignment has sent me to Europe's furthest corners, and each passing day I find myself longing ever more to return to you. Do you remember the old globe in the study? A trace of your finger due north-east from England and you will find Scandinavia, which is where I am at present. I had thought Petersburg was far enough! Fairlie has caused me much frustration; I confide I am incensed that he has sent me on this fruitless excursion as though my time was of such small value. Is the promise of promotion enough to see me through this? In the darker hours I feel I'd rather uproot and hunt for greener pastures. Work should never impede on home so negatively. This might just be a mistake that I have had to make so that my eyes may be opened. Still, the present situation is infuriating. Yet while the weeks apart now drift into months I wish for you to know of my unending devotion to you. I ache with every thought of your loveliness, my dear. Pray I may be by your side again sooner rather than later, when this winter finally ends and we can enjoy the summer back home. You must prevent your fool of a husband from undertaking such stupid tasks again!

All my heart belongs to you,

Pinnacle.

From the pen of Edythe Tricks;

My dear Pinnacle,

I told you this was a bad idea, that Fairlie was just using you to complete a task he did not want to do himself. Silly man. I jest of course, love, and cannot express in so many words how much I agree with your sentiments. Come home, my love. Your work shouldn't force a married man to be away from his wife for so long. Better to live simply and happily than to be wealthy and separated from those you love. I miss you too but know you are more than capable of dealing with anything put in front of you. Do not trouble yourself with a fear of ghosts and conspiracy. Things at home are fine. The cotton grass is starting to grow again; perhaps this winter is nearly over. I remember you always thought the cotton looked like spider webs. I've picked a few shoots to display in the kitchen window. They remind me of you.

Edythe.

From the pen of Ague Wight;

Mother,

We are LEAVING. I hate Thorn. I hate Papa for dying. I hate to leave you. They're taking me away from you. Why

can't I ever stay with you? Nobody listens to me. Thorn said we are going to London and didn't listen to me when I said that you were here and if we went to London we would leave you behind. I'll never forgive Thorn. Mother, will you come with us? *Can* you come with us?
Leaf.

From the diary of Hemlocke Wight;
I have my reservations about leaving home. I had fancied them to be the natural fears that come with moving into the oblivion of unknown, but maybe it is more to do with my doubting of mine own abilities. Father assigned me a task - it sounded simple enough at the time, but the arrival of this other man, this *Pinnacle Tricks* has thrown the entire situation into ordeal. What am I to do? Father's plan was foolish to me to begin with, and I can't shake the awkward dread that overcomes me to think of this new direction. It was actually Mr. Tricks' idea for us to go with him to London, where the matters at hand may be settled in person with Mr. Fairlie. I suppose there is little use in remaining here - I am still young enough to enjoy the fruits of youth, am I not? Mayhaps this is a step that must be taken, a pruning of old shoots that may blossom in abundance next spring. I have read that London is a grand city. Ague however, continues to vex me. Off in her fantasy land at all times; if only she would see clearly, then I might have someone to lean on during this horrible darkness. Oh sister please, I am doing my best. I don't know the answers to your questions. I don't know if we will return to the house. What does it matter? There is no reason for us to be here anymore. I want to feel something, anything other than the unending sadness that cloaks me.

XIV : Interlude
Helsinki, 1889

"Fate will unwind as it must!"
– Unknown (Beowulf).

There was a crack, and a sharp fissure cut its path into the frozen bay. Its echo jettisoned from the ice shelf in an attempt to find something to reverb against, but there was nothing. And just like the thick slabs of ice plunged into ocean, perhaps the echo would carry itself forever, lost in the sound of ever-moving waves, of restless seas awakening from sluggish Arctic slumber. The sharp crack sounded again, a new sonic tide chasing its elder in a futile race. Another block of ice slid into the sea, with none there to tell of Earth's yawning efforts to awaken. Perhaps a petrel wheeled into a somersault before continuing its flight; perhaps a crab clenched its pincers into a defensive stance. The intrusive thawing of the ice gathered momentum under the blinding northern sunlight, whose beams reflected kaleidoscopic patterns off of those disturbed icy shards - a fleeting beauty that quickly melted into the oozy mud beneath. The sea dribbled slowly shore-bound, caressing the icy sand and moss with the gentleness of a mother. Relax, she said, pay no mind to the thaw, to the pains of childbirth, it is but a natural occurrence; you remember it well from the last orbit, and soon enough the freeze will patch itself back together and bring a return to the Siberian solitude that is Winter. But for now the winter loosened its grip, the wind from the South brought with it a hope for reprieve for all that is above that last line of taiga. For a few months there would be warmth in those bleak shoals where the globe pivoted. The blistering sun saturated the ancient land of Thule. That warm wind coloured the bell-cry of the gulls, haunting the Siberian scene, where any man may wonder just how they could be so impossibly alone.

The ice-toothed bay thawed, the seals lay sleek in the midnight sun, and with this came the possibility of adventure, of ships taking to sea once more to escape to greener shores; the party that had gathered at Wight Estate were freed from the shackles of that old castle and, with a youthful refreshment that comes with Spring, worked their way towards Helsinki, to the port that would promise the outset of a new journey. Their caravan trundled along melancholic, imbued with a cautious optimism - each of its passengers brooding upon a different yet interlocked fate. For Pinnacle Tricks - his desires were plain to see, displayed on his sleeve, vulnerable and exploitable. He wished to be at home with his wife. And what man doesn't feel as he, when separated from one who holds him to a sturdy port, whose roots nourish a happy and comfortable life? Then there were the 'dryads', Ague and Hemlocke. Leaf and Thorn. One of straw and kindling, the other of midnight and mystery. The twin women held conflicted intentions; neither truly wanting to be going ahead with the journey to England, both having to adjust to the disruptions of their original plans. And what of Viy, the otherwise unnamed enigma? His desires appeared satisfied simply in the thrill of adventure, of being able to pen this chapter into the journal of his life. Having realised his services would no longer be required he had informed them of his intent to escort Tricks and the dryads to the harbour at Helsinki only, where Mr. Dergatsya had arranged a passage on a steamboat to take them to England. His promise to return to his wife had to be fulfilled, and unlike poor Mr. Tricks there were no chains withholding him from going home.

Pinnacle had received a single correspondence from his superior in Fairlie. The dismissive manner in which the letter appeared to be penned had riled the young man, whose homesickness had now fermented into a bitter frustration. If it had been *initiative* that Fairlie had wanted of Tricks, then he would take it upon himself to deliver the proprietors of Wight's will directly to his doorstep. The frivolous Dergatsya had experienced a similar silence from Ereven Fairlie that led him to agree with Tricks' idea to take matters back to London. Through the winter months he had prepared Ague and Hemlocke as best he could, explained through correspondence the steps required to resolve the matter of the will entirely, so that all parties could dust themselves of the affair and carry on with their individual existences. For the sisters, the risk lay in the complete upheaval of their lives as they knew them and the navigating of new territories. A chapter of their lives had been brought to a close, the page ripped from the book rather than simply turned, and both knew there would be no going back on this decision. Although some deliberation was imminent, Hem realised the importance of making such a drastic change, and to her relief Ague had put up little resistance. Whether this was her twin's intent or not remained unknown to Hemlocke, yet she would be gracious for the relative ease in which Ague had been coaxed along.

Still her sister had said little on the journey, instead listening to the serene sounds of the Finnish landscape for what could be the last time, and watching starry-eyed with wonder as Viy told nightly stories about their campfires. His stories often drifted towards the macabre; nightmarish tales of the Wendigo[40] and other horrifying creatures that are said to lurk in forests, to such an extent that both Pinnacle and Hemlocke would plead for him to tell of something more cheerful. Viy's stories,

---

[40] *Wendigo:* Mythical creature often depicted as a half-man, half-beast. A frighteningly savage monster usually associated with cannibalism.

fascinating though they were to Ague, filled the travellers with a lurking dread, one that hung just over their shoulders, out of sight even if one were to turn their head towards the darkness. The fire played tricks on them, casting flickering glows on the trunks of ancient trees where the owls would echo their sombre nocturne, giving the joyless fir cones the appearance of eyes; Pinnacle Tricks could not help but think of the will-of-the-wisp Viy had mentioned on their way to Wight Estate. Verily the flames of their campfire reflected menacingly off the eyes of forest creatures, off the dwindling patches of snow and in the cold, loveless stars above. The ghost lights, ever-watching - their gaze could not be shaken off. Alone, they were not, and Tricks could not quash thoughts of a certain sinister shadow that he felt was following them through the woods. Perhaps it was the cabin fever that came with the long winter still furnished him with paranoia, but on more than one occasion Tricks maintained with vehemence that something lurked just out of their sights in the tracks they had made, threatening to come forth at any moment and confirm its tangibility before bringing their desperate quest to an end. Once more he questioned his own sanity; the estate and its empty village had already brought to him images of wights and banshees, always twitching feverishly in his peripheral visions, so that he still doubted his very own eyes.

In the end it would not be Viy who provided reassurance but a surprising admonition from Hemlocke that reined in Tricks' fanciful doubts and brought him composure.

"These things you claim to see simply don't exist. Please, there is enough horror in life already; I know I certainly don't need any more turbulence. Stop looking behind you. There is nothing."

"Forgive me, Miss Wight," he replied, "I suppose homesickness breeds foolishness."

He felt oafish to have incited more grief than

needed, especially for Hemlocke and Ague, who had already suffered immeasurably at the loss of their parents and the leaving of the home they had always known - an exile from exile as it were.

"Follow, follow, here's a swallow," tittered Ague, "don't cry foul, it's just an owl…"

"Shush, Ague!" Hemlocke hissed.

"Leaf."

"*Ague!*"

"No," continued Ague, "leaf. Look!"

She held aloft an aspen leaf. Hemlocke grunted her frustration as her sister giggled louder still. Until then Viy had sat silently between them all, the reins of their horses held limply in his lap, but anon he too chuckled loudly, much to the distaste of the stormy Hemlocke.

"Well then, Viy," she grumbled, "we've heard little from you thus far that doesn't involve ghosts and monsters. And we've definitely heard enough of that. How about a story that might cheer us up instead?"

"Miss Wight, all my stories are fabricated from here," he tapped his balding scalp, "whether they be cheery or sullen matters little."

Hemlocke huffed, clapped her hands in her lap and gazed at the trees that slowly passed beside them.

"Perhaps," said Viy, "I could recite the poem I have been working on, but…"

"But?"

"But Miss Wight, though I call it finished I am not sure of its quality. For you see, I wrote it in English and this is not shall I say, my stronger tongue. I was merely thinking of the summer and thought to write of it."

"Let's hear it," said Tricks, "Lord knows any thought of summer would be relieving."

Viy hesitated, "As you wish, my friends. Let it be my parting gift to you."

He spoke:

The Will of the Wisp

Sun up -
The lily flowers open sweetly.
The stillness of the day insects betray.
Silent birds perch brooding in the shade;
In undergrowth the sweating lizards lay.

Sun set -
His name young Icarus[41] did scoff.
Bereft the day laments its faded azure.
Tenebrific bats repel the mourners,
Carried off by saintly nocturne measure.

Sun gone -
The luna crescent petals close.
Moon-scented glowing blossom incubates.
Dancing dryads peel petals anon.
The muse is born, the egg disintegrates.

Awake -
The ancient goblins through the fever
Frolic in the lingering heat of day.
Young dryads drink the stars with infant thirst,
And smell of grass entwines through their array.

Intrude -
The weary traveller staggers lost
And stumbles on this clandestine debut.
The dryads, they did scatter there like leaves
And awful silence permeated through.

The muse -
In puerile scorn did swiftly leer
And left the traveller quivering with fear.

---

[41] *Icarus:* Of Greek mythology. Icarus attempted to escape from Crete on wings made of wax and feathers; he fell to his death after flying too close to the sun, which melted his wings.

Away!
Her violet eyes aptly command.
The shivering man collapsed and couldn't stand.

Man wept -
And sin became too much to bear.
He prayed, sobbing, for a sunny morrow;
Wept to curtail joy and play perverse;
Wept to see such beauty hid from sorrow.

Where, then?
Could the man now hope to flee
After seeing things no man was meant to see?

How, then?
With this knowledge, could he be
Again within the company of the tree?

Wretched man!
His mind a sword of rust,
Still sharp enough to pierce a thieving mind
That tries to rob the world of mystery
And legend he was never meant to find.

Beware -
To wander in the woods at night
And see the goblins dancing in the vine;
One will see, in twisted, knotted wood
The man and muse forever locked in time.

Viy's words enraptured his companions - Pinnacle
shuddered with thoughts of sylvan[42] monsters and again
looked over his shoulders with the foreboding sensation of
being followed. Hemlocke had drifted into a peaceful

---

[42] *Sylvan:* Pertaining to woodlands, a spirit of the forest.

reverie before the poem's end brought forth her passions once more.

"That started cheerfully enough and still ended up being frightening!" She said.

Viy shrugged, "What is it they say? No blood can be drawn from a turnip?"

"I liked it," said Ague, "it reminded me of Mother."

Instead of scolding her sister Hemlocke caught her words and decided to let it be. Never mind that neither of them had known their mother, whom their father always said had perished in childbirth; Viy's words were elegant and full of mystique, there was no need to ground the mood with malice.

"Yes, I suppose I do feel the summer flourish in those words. Thank you and well done, Viy but -" said Hemlocke, "perhaps we can verse one another on happier thoughts until we reach the sea, what say you?"

Viy smiled, "Very well, Miss. Perhaps you can give it a title?"

Hemlocke thought for a moment but only seized up; any creative idea she might have had slipped from her mind and she could only stammer to fill the silence that only she was uncomfortable with. To her salvation came Ague, who perked in her seat with an insatiable smile.

"Lunatic!" She cried.

"*Cheerful*, Ague," laughed Hemlocke, "a *cheerful* title is what we need."

"I like it," said Viy.

"Yes, me too," Added Pinnacle.

And Hemlocke Wight could only sigh as the carriage continued on its way towards the harbour.

XV : Vanesther Bouclé
Paris, 1889

"Alas, it is better to wander in perpetual sterility than to be tortured with the remembrance of flowers that have withered."

- Charles Robert Maturin

Despite the rapidly drying oils crusted onto the wine-soaked palette, Vanesther Bouclé could not paint. The brush, held betwixt fingers slender and dexterous, quivered impatiently in her grasp. The canvas beneath repelled her advances almost magnetically, throwing insults at her through stitchings of blank, empty white. Verily all the elements were against her; the fine Parisian morning had turned overcast with the noon, her scant but expensive oils were drying faster than her apathy, and - worst of all - her mind was too cluttered to form any ideal worth expressing. Yet still her dusky brow furrowed, her antique hand remained aloft; she had taken the time to set up her easel, to pour the turpentine until its cloying smell filled her apartment, she could not give up now. The din of Saint-Germain-des-Pres drifted intrusively from below and into Vanesther's already distracted head, and all at once she threw the brush into the jar of turpentine and began to seethe behind a cigarette. The day was growing steadily worse; there came a wind through linden trees, and the dollops of cadmium yellow and burnt umber hardened to a crust, forever quelled of their chance to be a part of any magnum opus.

"The light is wrong to paint." she brooded.

Her coffee had gone cold. It was nearing the end of February, a bad month for Vanesther. That last booming cough of winter always had an adverse effect on her mood, regardless of any attempt she might have made to make things different. But, this time the February will be good. Tolerable, at least. Even so the thaw came to her home city of Paris, the Seine threatened to burst its banks and Vanesther felt sick with the damp of melted snow. It had been no different this year; just one more turn of the globe and she felt her beauty fade further in oblivion, albeit softening into an aged dignity.

"But I am not so old yet!" announced the quinquagenarian.

With the passing time, she had felt the burden of her failings grow heavier. Already she felt the pangs of artistic unfulfillment through the blank canvas sitting on the easel in the middle of her apartment. Her amber eyes scanned her homely furnishings. Her violin sat dusty with disuse in the corner; the strings had failed long ago and she had not bothered to replace them. At that moment she had doubts as to whether she still remembered any of Bach's preludes[43], or if the notes she once knew so well had drifted away with her mirth. Vanesther then felt herself to be a waste of talent, as she had done so many times, and followed this self-sabotage with paranoid thoughts of colleagues hating her, that whether she could paint or not didn't even matter anyway. She could smash her violin to kindling, striking at her canvases to land that second bird with the one stone, throw it all to the fire and sob wretchedly. While this would temporarily fill the artistic want and relieve the vents of frustration, soon enough that horrible sabotaging pressure would build again. Her soul was a leaking vessel, and nothing could staunch the bleeding from washing uselessly away.

Her legs cramped from their uncomfortable perch atop the wooden stool, and despite the monk-like discipline offered by an oppressive roost, she stood to

---

[43] *Bach's preludes:* Johann Sebastian Bach (1685–1750). German composer and musician.

stretch. Drawn to the window, her moth-wing shawl flapping the spectrum in graceful movements, she fully observed the grey sky for the first time that day, staring child-like against the full force of the increasing wind and deciding there and then that she would not be a martyr for artistic endeavour - not today, at least. The window was pulled closed, and although Vanesther felt somewhat relieved she still wrestled with the confines of her frustration. What she needed was fresh air; the dust settling in her home would not weigh her down any further. Against all precautions offered by the worsening weather she snatched her coat and scarf and escaped into the hallway, the wispy plume from her cigarette trailing behind her. The wooden steps in the foyer were steep, narrow and chilled to the bone, and Vanesther instantly felt winter's teeth like an onset of vertigo.

"Fool I am to be out on a day like this."

However, left bank was bustling with pedestrians. Vanesther could hear the Seine rumbling in the noise of wind, current and urban clutter - the lifeblood of Paris coiling its way betwixt the banks with the sleight of a snake and regality of a king. She breathed deep the air and shuddered at the needle touch inside her lungs, exhaling in sharp blows that were visible before her face. The pedestrians, as nameless as she on the sidewalk, there only to accentuate the finer details of this Parisian painting, scuttled with hermit-crab steps to unknown destinations, many of them were probably heading home and out of the oncoming storm. The clouds quivered overhead, fat with rain, yet Vanesther still walked. Where her feet were leading her she did not know, and she felt that she did not need to know.

She had subconsciously made her way to the Seine and now followed it like a blind man running his hand along a wall. All around the greens of market stalls, linden leaves and moss-coated stone lent a verdant freshness; a proclamation that spring was marching forth and would soon arrive at the gates of Paris. Gypsies jangled their wares in her face with exclamations that were pleading and intrusive.

Buy! They said. *Consume! Partake!*

Vanesther only gritted her teeth and declined, cursing their desperation that interrupted her sombre thought train.

"Joli collier pour une jolie dame?"[44]

"Non monsieur."

The onslaught of trinkets, of sketches, of jewellery and books filled Vanesther with that longing to paint that had hitherto been missing and though she did not buy (only observed, as the artist often does), she consumed the creative fuel that the green-stalled merchants provided. Down by the riverside she spied a black cat staring absently at its own reflection, and even that accentuated her flairs of whimsy, leading her to think that maybe she *was* an artist after all.

In a more fanciful state of mind, I'd see that as an omen.

The further she walked the more her frustration flew from one perch to another, and by the time she reached Pont Neuf, Vanesther felt that yes, she could paint again, but was she not too old to leave her mark on the world? She cast her mind back to the days of her youth, when paint flowed like water and the worriment that came with aging materials and wasted paints did not phase her; days when she still knew her husband, an Englishman named Brishen Garrick who had become enrapt in her ethereal beauty, in the dusky mystique that enveloped the young female artist.

How do you know when to paint? he would say, *What if good paint is wasted on something that doesn't turn out* just *the way it needs?*

Vanesther was always flippant in her response; *one can*

---

[44] *"Joli collier pour une jolie dame?":* French – "Pretty necklace for a pretty lady?"

remain steadfast for years, only to splurge on one indulgent moment.

She felt now that she knew the meaning of the statement even more. With a twinge of sadness she recalled her husband, lost to the Crimean War all those years ago. She recalled how the money had flowed away faster than her grief, how she would stop at nothing to paint over the raw despair that his death served. Paint was of little worth trapped in those tubes, yet the meagre income all artists seem doomed to remain trapped with meant that great care needed to be taken as to when her more expensive paints were used. When Vanesther had received the news that her husband was missing, presumed dead, a part of her would waste away and never return. Her restraint went to the winds and with her life offering little else of value she squandered whatever money she and her husband had built over the years. There was a seed of panic that grew in Vanesther's stomach, a seed watered with a fear of failing that urged her to fulfil whatever calling she had. Fear and melancholy clouded her imagination, pushed her down paths that led to nowhere, and as such her critics shook their heads and lamented her 'wasting talent'. Bereft, Vanesther would cry in the night as the dust collected in her broken home. The only portrait of her husband would serve as a martyr for her private anguish, his caricature locked in a sepia smile that she would never again see in the flesh.

Do you know what they said of me? Pretentious. Oh, that word struck my heart like an earthquake. Do you see this lady standing before you as pretentious? These poor lodgings? Remark not of my eloquence of speech, for that is something even you said we all should strive for. No, I will not compromise that. Oh Brishen, why do you stare at me like that? I've failed my calling! If a true artist can deal with criticism then perhaps I never was one to begin with. Am I melodramatic? How can I know? I've no-one left.

Her musing had led Vanesther to a cafe on Rue-Saint Jacques, where she pilfered through her pockets for coins and ordered a café noisette[45]. It still had not rained, although the sky threatened with rumblings of thunder and gusts of wind. The newspaper stands on the street side fluttered on the flurries of wind, and Vanesther thought she could smell the ink that had been laid out in words that people would understand. The cafe was a delight to her senses; mahogany walls stood stained with the aroma of a thousand-fold coffees and the tables, green and white, groaned beneath the elbows of the patrons. Vanesther rapped her nails against the table top and allowed the scent of coffee to wash over her, falling again into a state of melancholic musing.

Coffee this late? I suppose I wouldn't have slept tonight, anyway.

And she knew even then that her insomniac tendencies were her own doing. The thought nagged at her, but she ignored it as she always did. She had heard it said that the harshest critic is one's self, and Vanesther could only groan inwardly and wonder how she could ever hope to win that fight.

I know I am stubborn, yet this demon in me, this critic, *feels like a thousand-man army. And there I stand, alone on my little hill waving my colours. Is the flag white? It may as well be. Perhaps I am still beautiful, but I know I am no longer as strong as I once was. Unlike an immortal portrait I've grown old; the paint has cracked with age, any assets I had have become over-abundant, and this smile that could once win any man over has contorted into wrinkled disarray. Brishen, what ever happened to you? What did they do to you?*

Leaving behind a smattering of cigarette ash and some dirty coins in the ashtray, Vanesther resumed her walk. She would have to head back home soon; the weather was not going to hold much longer. Sleet began to fall sporadically in mean drops as the sky took on an ethereal glow - a glow that appears only when cloud cover is heavy, and the sun's smothered light seems to shine in the opposite direction.

---

[45] *Café noisette:* Espresso served with hot milk. French – literally 'hazelnut coffee', referring to its colour.

On a sudden Vanesther felt as though it could still be morning even though the afternoon was certainly giving itself over to dusk. The conflict of summer thunder with winter sleet confused her, and verily the day itself didn't know what it wanted to be. The air filled with the carnivalesque notes of a busker whose accordion breaths might have created the wind itself, as the instrument bellowed out an archaic and wheezing dirge. There weren't too many people left in the streets by then. The vampish horrors of the night began to gather in the awnings of shops and clumped in piles of garbage that haunted the alleys. Any fools still wandering the streets had outstayed their welcome, and the city of Paris, the city of lights, made sure those fools knew it.

Vanesther closed the door to her flat and exhaled an ecstatic sigh of relief. One more day she'd survived, and although that still meant another night in isolation, she had done enough to keep her saboteurs at bay. Only then did she notice just how dark it had become during her outing - the canvas still stood there, empty, yearning. Tapping the palette's hardened paint dollops with her fingers she cursed. They probably couldn't be saved. All around her the catalogue of unfinished paintings cowered from their master. Some had been an idea run dry, others had been imagination cut short by paint tubes emptied too soon with no money to replace them. Vanesther lit a few candles and sat in her more comfortable chair, her dark curls falling aimlessly about the armrests as she rested her feet on the oppressive stool.

No sitting vigil on that damned stool tonight.

She lit another cigarette and inhaled deeply, savouring the silence and her own personal loneliness, knowing true well that Paris continued to bleed outside her window. She would have probably fallen asleep there until morning, until a knock on the door broke her trance. Vanesther cursed again - cursed the interruption, cursed the fear that crept in her heart *(who would call by at this hour?)* and cursed the stool that fell over when she stood. The spyglass revealed the features of an old man she didn't quite recognise, but once the fishbowl perspective of the spyglass was replaced with her own amber eyes, her heart fell to her floor at the open door. She would later wonder how the rest of her remained standing as a desperate gasp escaped her lips in the form of a single word.

"Faron...."

The man stood expectantly, his hands in his pockets, head bowed like guilty dog.

"Ness," he said, "May I come in?"

Vanesther stood aside - *I am letting a ghost into my house.*

"I go by Ereven, now," said the man, "Ereven Fairlie."

XVI : North Sea
Off Jutland, 1889

"Dark clouds bring waters, when the bright bring none."
– John Bunyan

"Hold fast, there, boy!"

"I'll kill us, pa!"

Still the boy clutched the wheel of the steamer as his grandfather instructed, praying for the colossal berg off the port side to glide silently by them. His heart felt tight in his chest, the blood pumping thick as syrup, throbbing violently in his ears. Surely he could not fail from here. Although the miles between them and the Nordic shore would make their survival impossible in the event of shipwreck, it was in fact the fear of disappointing his grandfather and captain that frightened him. The floes slid by eel-slick in the grey sea, and when the last and most massive berg sidled by the boy let out a sigh of relief, his heart rate returning to a steady thrum. He fancied he could almost see the sun cutting weakly through the clouds and down onto the decks, illuminating his fortunate victory over Neptune's[46] realm, although that may have just been a fancy of his childish mind.

"There, Oddbergur!" Laughed his grandfather, "Like a professional, my boy!"

Oddbergur smiled but said nothing.

Stout and august Cedrus Festoon pressed his big hands against the forward rail and breathed deep of the salty air. His wind-tossed body stood defiant against the tide; only the salt-crusted wool of his pullover and the

---

[46] *Neptune*: Roman God of the sea.

worn cotton of his coat quivered about his otherwise immovable stance. His face cracked with a bittersweet age, the crow's feet around his eyes displaying the aftermath of a thousand smiles. He wore a warm demeanour on that face, a *joie de vivre*[47] that had proved more than infectious to those fortunate enough to have conversed with him over the years. Eftsoons he turned to his grandson, who was still shaking about the wheel of the steamer and gave him a triumphant fist pump. The boy returned the gesture before reapplying his focus on the horizon ahead.

Eyes forward; don't turn your back to the sea for an instant.

Oddbergur knew the rules - how could he forget? Cedrus had plugged such notions to him from the time he could walk; now nearing his eleventh birthday, most of Reykjavik had heard of the local boy whose sea legs had sprouted faster than the white dryads[48] in summer. The ocean was a heartless thing, beautiful and deadly, and demanded a cautious respect from those that sought passage across her.

"With Jutland behind us now it should be full steam ahead, my boy."

"I hope the crew weren't too shaken by all that."

"Haw! They are seasoned sailors, lad. I'd be more concerned about our land-lubbing passengers, haw haw! Aww don't look like that boy! Even the finest helmsman this side of the Atlantic would have struggled through those floes."

Cedrus entered the bridge and clapped the boy on the shoulder, "Wait until your Grandmother hears about that one!"

Oddbergur felt a warmth in his chest; his grandmother was a most kindly woman whom he missed

---

[47] *Joie de vivre*: French – literally 'joy of life'.
[48] *White dryads*: Floral emblem of Iceland, Oddbergur's home country.

dearly. Whether he'd piloted a ship or merely tied his own shoes she was always beaming with pride. Yet it would be a long time before they made port and returned home to her.

"Right then, lad," said Cedrus, "Enough daydreaming. I'll take it from here. How's about you check up on the mob down in the cabins. See if they're still holding their lunch in their bellies!"

The boy scratched his nose, stretched his back and swung his arms to and fro as Cedrus clasped the mahogany wheel.

"Time to eat, Pa."

"Ha! Patience, lad. Ask nicely and maybe Mr. Tricks will cook you up a feed like last night."

"Gran says I've got to grow," Here he pushed his miniscule belly out as much as he could; "Don't want to be getting scurvy."

"You well-fed rascal. I may not be able to cook like your Gran but I keep you alive out here - don't you be forgetting!"

"I won't, Pa." replied the boy, as he tore off down the deck towards the guest quarters.

Nightfall still came early in the Spring, the sun's twilit rays shone weakly on the grey sea like spot fires, blurring the line where sea ended and sky began. Oddbergur had not gone immediately to the guest cabins as his grandfather had requested, rather he spent the better part of the afternoon distracted by a blue shark that was lazily tailing the steamer. He was not a disobedient boy but was easily distracted; it would appear that the effort exerted in steering the ship earlier had exhausted all the mental capacity he could afford for the day. He did, however, hold a respectable fear of his elders, and when the blue shark grew bored of following the boat and turned away, Oddbergur snapped to attention and made a speedy beeline towards his original destination. The cabins below deck were cramped at best - never an issue to Cedrus and his motley crew - now that they had several passengers though the confines seemed to close in tighter around them. For Oddbergur, he couldn't recall a time when the ship was so full of life. Personally he enjoyed the company, though he would not admit it, for *boys should be tough* as his father used to say, *and need little but themselves for company.* He never truly stopped to consider what those words had meant, even though they parroted in his brain more often than necessary. Not that it mattered now, midway betwixt Norway and Britain on his grandfather's vessel. He snatched at the telescope hung on a nearby wall and burst headlong into the tiny cabin hallway, where he came awfully close to knocking over Hemlocke Wight, who was strolling up from the other direction.

"Hoy, Miss Hem!"

Hemlocke glared down at the bulbous eye blinking through the end of the telescope before pushing her anger aside. She couldn't be cross with the boy, he was only young. The lady looked completely out of place on board the ship, dressed in a smock and gown that was too fancy for the seafaring. Not that she had much to go on; this was the furthest she and Ague had ever ventured from their dark towers in Lapland.

This boy is half my age and has seen more of the world than I.

"Hello, young man. Where are you heading to in such a hurry?"

"Your hair looks like seaweed!" Laughed Oddbergur.

Hemlocke's jaw dropped indignantly.

"He is only joking." Ague popped her head out from behind the cabin door.

"Y-yes. Indeed," replied Hem, "Well. *Your* hair looks like an owl struck by lightning."

"Well that would be pretty amazing to survive a lightning strike... But right now I'm just hungry."

Hemlocke grunted disdainfully, "Ugh, little parasite. Why don't you go bother Pinnacle; he is out on the deck drawing."

Oddbergur gave her a cheeky salute and raced back out onto the deck. Heading aft to where he had been watching the blue shark, he saw Pinnacle Tricks seated with his pencils and drawing book, the wake trailing the steamer carrying white ribbons off into the horizon. By now the sun was well and truly gone; only the watercolour wash of twilight remained. The boy crept up behind Tricks to observe his drawing, but Tricks, feeling the presence of somebody behind him, jumped up on a sudden.

"My, Oddbergur, you startled me."

"Doesn't take much to do that, no?"

"I-I guess not."

"Can I see your drawing?"

"Certainly, not much I'm afraid - just sketches." Said Tricks, allowing Oddbergur to flip through the pages.

"I must say," added Pinnacle, "that your grandfather made a good subject without even realising it! That's him leaning over the back rail there."

He pointed to the paper - on it was a monochrome seascape of a man staring out at the sea from the deck of a ship. It had taken him some time to complete, out of practice with his arts as he was, and once he had enjoyed a small moment of pride he looked up and saw the puzzled look on Oddbergur's face.

"Something the matter, son?"

He watched as Oddbergur looked towards the stern of the ship, then to the bow, then back at Tricks.

"Pa is up there at the wheel," he said, "has been all day."

The expression on Tricks' face changed to that of bemusement, and he raised his gaze to the empty stern of the ship, where the shadowy figure he had been sketching earlier was no longer there. Feeling his mouth go dry, he stammered for words but his brain would not allow it.

"Yo? Mr. Tricks?"

"I'm sorry?"

"I said that Pa has been at the bridge today. Couldn't be him at the stern there."

"I see. Perhaps some other ship hand, then."

"Doubt it. They spend their days manning the engines. I reckon Pa would scold them good if he caught 'em lollygagging on the decks."

"Ah yes, of course."

I'm going insane.

Tricks had run into more than enough superstitious activity of late that he had begun to doubt his own mind. The need to be chastised back to reality had been called upon too often by those he had met on his adventure - Viy, Oddbergur, even that cat in the Ignis Errand Inn! There had to be more to it; he had lived his entire life with little more than passing thought to the idea of ghosts and goblins, yet this venture to Russia and back had derailed much of the sensibility he had thought he possessed. How much of it had been fabrication? How much of it had been tangible? The light had been fading. Yes, that must explain the figure in his sketch.

I have always been a logical man - my father made sure of that.

And the ghosts of Wight's village? The shadows of the Petersburg inn? Figments of the imagination. Never had Pinnacle been away from home for such a period of time. Surely that would have been enough to mess around with his mindset. Best to keep the mind on homely things, and with the young lad Oddbergur standing expectantly by his side, Pinnacle realised it was time for him to cook them their evening meal.

****

The cramped walls of the sweating kitchen were a stark contrast to the brisk airs above deck, yet its warmth offered a sense of homeliness that struck a pleasing balance with the sense of adventure provided by the sea spray and ocean breeze. When the hours of the day had made the men weary they could retire to a place closer to the luxuries of home - save the unfortunate sailor drawn to night watch in the crow's nest. That loveless task had fallen to poor young Oddbergur on that particular evening, so while he sat green-eyed and seething atop the mast, haunch frozen with the winds whistling about the crow's nest like a tuning fork, the rest of the crew sat jovially and patiently awaited the evening meal from their unlikely chef. Pinnacle Tricks had been a salvation to the homesick sailors; his ability to conjure up a decent feed from meagre resources had earned him favour with Cedrus and the crew. With Viy having parted ways with them at Helsinki, it had fallen to Tricks to provide, with both Hemlocke and Ague being unfortunately lacking of culinary skill. Although the sisters had tried to help, their sheltered lives had left them ill-equipped in a number of crucial basics, and often things would turn all the worse for their efforts. Still that evening it was mostly the efforts of Tricks, who, between the stirring of pots kept a wary eye on Ague, busied by the duties of chopping onions. Something about the wispy girl holding a sharp utensil filled Pinnacle with angst, angst that yoked both he and Hemlocke together, for she too questioned her sister's integrity. One strong jolt and that knife could fly anywhere.

"Oh Ague, stop crying." huffed Hemlocke.

"Tis the onions." she moped, wiping her face with the very same hand that brandished the knife. Pinnacle winced as it brushed sickeningly close to Ague's sallow cheek.

"Ye habits are concerning," said Cedrus, "but p'raps I've been at sea too long."

"Oh I don't know how to cook! How should I?" Here Ague threw the knife point down into the chopping block, where it shuddered like a loosed arrow. Pinnacle moved quickly to remove the utensil from her reach.

"Not you, sweet pea," continued Cedrus, "but your sister."

Hemlocke looked abashed, greatly disliking unwarranted attention, "Me? What ever can you mean?"

Cedrus took on an expression of fatherly concern, "Yer food goes mostly untouched, and yer getting thinner by the day!"

"Well thank you for the concern," she replied indignantly, "but I am just fine; chalk it up to a touch of seasickness, I suppose."

"Aye, will take some time to be used to it, lass," said Cedrus, "I mean ye no harm, pardon my intrusiveness I s'pose."

Although the discussion ended there, one point continued to press upon Pinnacle Tricks; Hemlocke hadn't been eating much; very little at all, considering the length of their journey. Initially putting it down to a bird-like appetite, Tricks thought nothing of it, yet the question remained as to what became of her share of meals.

Superstitious fool, she is probably just spacing out her consumption to stave away the seasickness. Yes, that must be it.

His mind would not be settled and, despite the bitter cold howling above deck, he stepped out to give Oddbergur his company on the crow's nest.

Oddbergur sat benumbed in the North Sea night, the darkness of which cloaked the dark wood of the mast and gave the impression of the boy floating in a barrel through a sea of stars. Although the wind was not as fierce as it had been at other stages of their journey, it still howled loudly enough to silence Pinnacle's approach, so that Oddbergur jolted from his daze upon his arrival atop the rope ladder.

"Mr. Tricks! Hoy, you startled me."

"Never mind, lad. Consider it payment for you doing the same to me this afternoon."

Pinnacle sat next the boy in the cramped barrel of

the crow's nest, unpacking the contents of a small sack containing morsels of food for the famished young boy.

"Cor, bless you, Sir." said Oddbergur, snatching a crust of bread and devouring it ravenously.

Tricks gazed into the overwhelming darkness. The steamer careened into the pitch, bound for a horizon lost betwixt the black of sky and ocean. Were he to squint and focus, Tricks imagined he could see that point where sea ended and sky began, but he could not be certain, such was the opacity of the night. An encompassing dread cascaded over his shoulders, and he was filled with horrors of shipwreck, of icebergs emerging into view far too late to steer around. Oddbergur, as though he were reading the thoughts of his companion, chirped gaily from his perch, "Pa always steers us through the night."

Crumbs sprayed from his mouth with that crude oblivion acceptable only with children, "Might be old but still sees great."

"Yes," replied Tricks, "well we're all the luckier for his skill; I can't see a thing."

"*Second set of eyes is always needed*, says my Pa," said Oddbergur, "I wish I could go inside though."

"I think we've all a place we'd rather be, son."

"Yeah, like Barcelona. Pa says it's hot as hell but I wouldn't know. Maybe I'll go there someday."

Tricks sighed, "I'd just like to be at home with my wife. Lord how I miss her and the comforts of home. I can't help but feel I've missed so much in being away this long."

"Then why'd you do it?"

"Hmm? You mean travel? I had supposed it would advance my career prospects; short term pain, long term gain. But now I realised being with those you love is far more valuable."

"Probably should have thought of that before you left." said Oddbergur.

Pinnacle laughed, "Hindsight is a wonderful thing,

my friend."

Oddbergur didn't know what hindsight was and didn't care to ask; he was far too engaged in eating his coveted dinner to listen further.

"You got through that quickly." Pinnacle remarked.

"I get so hungry at sea," said Oddbergur, "the food is so boring and I never feel full."

"Hemlocke had a portion left over. She declined to leave it for you, I'm afraid to say."

Several minutes passed, filled with an empty silence between the two of them; a few late gulls cried eerily through the darkness as the sound of wake crashed against the prow of the ship. It was enough to send Pinnacle into a trance, the gentle rhythm of the scene, the shocking cold, and soothing hush lulling him into blood-slowed fatigue. Yet a curious sound would stomp into earshot; the thunk of a closing door piquing the attention of Pinnacle and Oddbergur. Peering over the barrel they observed Hemlocke, dressed still in that flowing dress (which had to be frightfully cold at the current hour) emerge from a discrete trap door in the foredeck. She moved with a stealthy purpose, looking each way carefully and threading her way softly around the ropes and barrels that littered the bow. She moved with the haunting grace of a ghost and, assuming nobody had seen her, slipped back through the main doors into the cabins below deck.

"D'you suppose she sleep walks?" came Oddbergur's voice. Pinnacle pondered momentarily, "Very peculiar."

He looked to his companion and relaxed his furrowed brow into a gaze of compassion, for Oddbergur held the look of a child shocked awake by a nightmare.

"I've heard stories of people going mad at sea," Oddbergur whispered, "There are ghosts in these waters. Dragon ghosts that can sink us. Blimey, Mr. Tricks, what if they've possessed Miss Hem and she plans to wreck us?"

"I highly doubt that, Oddbergur."

"How do you know? You only met her just before I did! What if she's a banshee?"

"You are overthinking this, son," said Pinnacle, "it was merely Hemlocke - no ghost or ghoul - and I am certain she has reason for being on deck at this hour. Remove such silly fancies from your mind."

Still, there would be no relief for Pinnacle Tricks. Despite his words grounding Oddbergur's childish ideas, he was unable to tackle his own paranoia, and the strange behaviour of his companions Hemlocke and Ague only increased his uneasiness. The steamer continued on its way to England, and Tricks felt relief at the thought of his approaching home, hoping it would bring with it a resolution to his strange adventure. An approaching of Hemlocke resulted in a vehement denial that anything was amiss, and although her peculiar habits continued unabated, Tricks himself saw his interest wane with each setting sun. Thoughts of the strange voices he had heard at Wight Estate vanished like the ghosts he thought he'd seen; presumptions of unnamed figures emerging from the corners of his eyes returned to the shadows from whence they had come. The days blurred together as he tried to push away thoughts of suspicion, or homesickness, and he oft had the recurring thought that he had wandered into a spider's web, where he must carefully attempt to free himself without provoking the attention of a most sinister predator. Pinnacle cared no longer to understand the full details behind Mr. Fairlie's intentions; he cared only for his feet to plant themselves onto home soil. Aware that life held mysteries that he was not meant to understand, he resigned himself to the fate that drove him closer to where he began, where he would be left to wonder the entire purpose of the sojourn and when this unusual chapter of his life would come to a close.

XVII : London Revisited

"Slept, awoke, slept, awoke, miserable life."
-     Franz Kafka

Atlas Egerton didn't quite understand the situation. Not that he would; was there ever a time where he had been kept in the loop with such matters? It was better not to think of it. After all, he had his own demons to deal with. Yet his master's reaction to a certain letter - another from young Pinnacle Tricks - was one that caused him to shudder on recollection. Atlas had not read the letter himself, and could only make assumptions of its details from Fairlie's less than composed reaction to it. He had watched the colour drain from his master's face, seen the sweat break out on his brow as the paper quivered in the old man's grasp. Atlas had been dismissed almost immediately and the ever-astute servant was obligated to comply.

Had some ill fate befallen Pinnacle? He had to doubt this. Loyal as he was to his superior, Atlas had never known Fairlie to show much concern to his fellow man, and he had high doubts that a cold-hearted man such as Fairlie would react with such alarm to a transpiratory such as that. The reluctance towards the mission had been apparent in Pinnacle's heart right from the beginning, and in all honesty the situation was perplexing. This strange character, this Mr. Wight - his request that his will be settled in person between his lawyer and Fairlie was, to Atlas at least, redundant and unnecessary. Surely it was a matter that could be settled through correspondence alone, and even if the situation demanded the presence of the benefactor, why involve poor old Tricks? Indeed there had been trepidation in Fairlie's own reaction to the news of Wight's death, refuting all suggestions that *he* go and settle affairs in Saint Petersburg in lieu of Tricks. No, he would not do it himself, all respects aside. If Wight had felt the need to leave the estate to him, so be it - that did not change Fairlie's sentiments towards him. Atlas felt for Pinnacle, wet behind the ears as he was he would no doubt learn a lot from the adventure.

"The boy could use a spine." Fairlie had said of Pinnacle, and Atlas agreed, but more in a sense that Pinnacle should get a backbone strong enough to say 'no' to his superior. In the end the entire situation had been handled poorly and, being the resolute servant that he was, Atlas Egerton had not spoken out on how *he* might have managed it better.

There had to be something more to that Mr. Wight. Of this mysterious spectre, Atlas had gleaned little information. He would recall such rare times over his years of servitude where Fairlie had received correspondence from the man, but any prying into who this man might be would always be met with a similar dismissive response.

"An old acquaintance from the army," he would mutter, his piercing eyes remaining fixed on the letter at hand, and his scolding tone subtly reminding Atlas to pursue with no further questions.

Other occasions where the man was mentioned by Fairlie were rare, but always carried with them a certain weight; a black cloud of despondency would encroach upon him on the speaking of his name. Fairlie had always been a private man - never one to share more than necessary, a trait which found him with few who would call them his friend - this trope betrayed that there was clearly a bitter history between he and Wight. Why else would his composition change so much at the mention of one man? For Atlas, the only history he had of his superior was that which accumulated over the seventeen years he had served under him. Any event that Fairlie had traipsed through before that (aside from his seldom-mentioned war days) was an utter mystery to him.

Atlas Egerton had asked himself the question - why had this Wight fellow left his estate to Fairlie, a man who, for all intents and purposes, clearly despised him? Did some blood-tie entitle him to such a prize? Had some wartime treaty fallen into his favour? Atlas found himself entertained by macabre thoughts of Faustian[49] deals, of souls sold to devils and greed that conquered piety.

Something that you would want belonging to you…

The simple yet sinister note left for Fairlie in Mr. Wight's will. It carried with it the weight of suspicion, a clandestine taunt that was understood in a context known only to Wight and Fairlie. Speculation bred lies though, and Atlas knew the danger of assumption. There was however, an itch that would not be satisfied, which begged the age-old question of heart over mind - was he wrong or right in following a suspicion grounded merely on a gut feeling? In a move that only further compounded this, Ereven Fairlie had flown from his coop almost instantly. Atlas had awoken the next morning to a somewhat febrile commotion about the estate and the news that Mr. Fairlie had 'stepped out to attend to certain business matters'. Hurt to have not been told this news personally (for he was, after all, Fairlie's longest-serving steward); Atlas Egerton soon shifted his focus towards corralling the other servants into line. Surely, their master was absent, but he would expect his home to be orderly upon his return. In the issuing of this order, Atlas had achieved two things; he had becalmed the *tabula rasa*[50] that was the minds of such household servants, and in doing so had shouldered their burden as well as his own, to where he could only click his

---

[49] *Faustian:* Of German folklore. Faust surrendered his soul in a pact with the devil in exchange for peerless knowledge.
[50] *Tabula rasa:* Latin – literally 'blank slate'. Used to describe a mind unaffected by experience or impressions, etc.

tongue and bemoan at their simple ignorance. He loathed to be forced into such decisions, for again he had taken the straight and narrow path that was paved with trial. His faith in his fellow man so lacking that he found himself without a yoke - he was on his own, and one could be forgiven for thinking he'd slip into the depths of despondency. Yet as suffering produces character[51], so too did Atlas channel his burden into his poetry. That one outlet he afforded to himself runneth over, and his opus *Gull and Leviathan* gilded itself with some of his finest thoughts refined.

Eventually the questions of his master's whereabouts and the secrecy of his mission began to plague him, smothering artistic inspiration and clouding his *raison d' être*[52]. Atlas realised that the letter from Pinnacle Tricks must have been a harbinger of things to come, like the first frost of late autumn, and although the clime was becoming summerly, he felt that shuddering forbearance that heralds the arrival of winter, of darkness. The clouds of doomed fate gathered over London, and came to a head one humid and dreary afternoon when the mighty oak doors of Fairlie's estate thundered with an echoing knock. Pinnacle Tricks had returned, bringing with him the kin of that mysterious Mr. Wight, to which Atlas Egerton could only shake his head and inform the young man that his master was not here.

---

[51] *Yet as suffering produces character…:* Paraphrase of Romans 5:3–5.

[52] *Raison d'être:* French phrase meaning 'reason for being'.

XVIII : Vanesther & Fairlie

"Who, being loved, is poor?"

-     Oscar Wilde

Vanesther's life had been shaken to its foundations in a single moment. The silent, moonlit arrival of her past-personified patiently awaited her acknowledgement. He knew the shock his appearance had caused, that the blockage of thought and questions that came with it would need time to process, like too much water flowing through a dam. Ereven Fairlie (or Faron, as Vanesther had addressed him) allowed the woman's eyes to soak in his stature, widened as they were like drops in a pool, stunned yet unable to dismiss the visitor as mere spectre. Her cigarette hung limply on her lip, the train of ash creeping slowly toward extinguishment so much that the man gestured carefully that she might catch it in time. Vanesther blinked, snapping back into reality and crushing the butt into the ashtray, before immediately lighting another.

"I understand my arrival might come as a bit of a shock."

"Yes. Shock."

Was it really him? Ravaged by age, answering to a pseudonym, but all there in the flesh - Faron Silas. A man Vanesther had known in her youth as her husband's best comrade. A man she had safely assumed had died in the war alongside her beloved Brishen. Thirty-five years had passed since she had laid eyes on either of them.

"Faron…"

"… Is not my name any longer. It has been this way since I returned to England many years ago,"

"But why? The war, Brishen. Brishen!" Vanesther gasped, "Tell of my husband!"

Fairlie shook his head, "I will get to that in time if you allow me to speak. I regret to say he won't be making an appearance such as mine."

"How are you here? And why? Gods, what is happening?" Vanesther sat down in the chair that had not long ago been a source of comfort for her. Her mouth was dry and she gained no satisfaction from her smoking. Fairlie strode slowly towards her and ensconced on the wooden stool so that he had to look up to see her.

"There are many things to say, Ness, and the reasons for my arrival - again I will get there. Suffice to say that there is so much more to what you know about the past thirty-five years. There has been, in my life, in Brishen's life, the influence of a man who drifts closer to daemon than human. A man, his name Walpole Wight - who must regrettably be the protagonist of my forgotten tale, but the cornerstone to my past, and my intentions for the future. Have you the ears to listen at present?"

Vanesther exhaled in a fluster and shrugged with bemusement, "Be my guest. This night certainly is not getting any stranger."

"I hope, yet doubt, that will be the case."

****

"It had become a quiet life. Our village lay in a bleak and bedraggled country in Lapland - far to the north, wild with the spidery tendrils of brambles, where the pines towered ominously and the cold cut with the sharpness of a sword. Some sinister air of unease hung about the place in swathes, reminding me always of those melancholic engravings of Gustave Doré[53] (I assume, my dear, that you still pursue your love of the arts). It was this unease that

---

[53] *Gustave Doré:* (1832–1883) French artist and illustrator.

tangled the cognition of the villagers we lived with that left
the settlement mired in the opaque reaches of some more
primitive time. A more modern man might have chuckled
at its furnishings; at its daemon-fearing citizens, at its garlic
wreaths hung in ramshackle kitchens, of beads and
crucifixes and other idols clutched fearfully to sallow
chests. The villagers lived their simple lives working the
muddy earth, reaping minimal harvest for their brutal
efforts while the castle towered over them on up the hill.
Brishen, I regret to say, was no longer with me at this
point. Walpole Wight sat his throne, yet his kingly stance
was contradicted by the almost schoolboy nature of his
attitude towards the villagers who worked for him. Like a
child stomping on ants he would laugh at them, took
delight in their ignorance; such cruel dictatorship flaunted
the awful skills that had earned him such high rank in the
British army, for that was the connection that led to our
initial liaison with him. He taunted the townsfolk with the
threat of curses - his presence so foreign to them that they
saw him as some enigmatic prophet. An obvious
advantage with his superior knowledge of the world, he
was able to build for himself - over years mind you - a
community where he was at the apex, with none who
would oppose him, all the while the townsfolk scurried
about below providing succour for his lavish albeit
minimal life.

I say that none could oppose him - rather I should
say that none could logically best his wit and wisdom. He
held his realm in a grip tighter and colder than that of the
winter. I've painted a bleak picture, an unenviable
existence, and you might ask why a man of his stature and
talents would have subjected himself thusly. It was only
there that we could forget the lives we once led and,
perhaps more importantly, be forgotten by those that once
knew us. Deserting the war never sounded appealing to
either of us; Wight in particular carried the thought with a
repulsed dread. For it could be said without question that

he had more to lose. I was nothing in this native land; was but a simple soldier with only a few stray friends to mourn of my death (forgive me this much, Vanesther). Tragic though this may seem, sympathy is not what I seek. You and I know I was never a good man. Upstanding qualities have crept into my persona at varying times of my life, but in a pinch I have always done what is best for myself and myself alone. I make no apologies for this. It is a short few years that I wander this earth - why anybody would waste them on piety, I have no idea. Perhaps this was why I had no problem deserting the army. Wight, as I said before that little introspective digression, had much to lose in way of stature. He was a venerable leader, a feared tactician. Stories of his mighty home in London passed their way through the rumblings of other soldiers like myself. Yet he would compromise all of this to preserve his facade of leadership. By the time we became separated from the platoon, we both knew we were on the losing side, and to feign death in battle was far more heroic a choice than surrendering. He never doubted that he could rebuild, and to his credit that is exactly what he had done.

****

But perhaps I am skipping over a few vital things. My apologies, it is difficult to collate so many years into a story. It must have been fate that brought us together. I will admit we both were cowards, Wight and I, and upon the day when I took refuge from the fight in those forest of Wallachia, I had no idea of the horrors my life would wander into. And here is where Brishen, the dearest (and only?) friend I've known made a pact with me - we would flee together. Neither of us cared at that moment where we ended up. Anywhere was better than the battlefield, although for Brishen, he ached for you. Longed desperately to be back here with you. It was this love he had for you that undoubtedly drove him to executing our plan. I don't know that anyone saw us slip from the platoon, but stumbling across our commander, Walpole Wight, in those trees led us to believe our escape had immediately been thwarted. I of course knew the man when I saw him, and expected all the lashes and punishment awaiting those who took such a godless path as we did. But there was a fear in Wight's eyes, and it took a moment for Brishen and I to realise that Wight too had harboured a desertion. That we had all formulated our plan, and executed it at the very same time - indeed it had to be fate that we met there and then.

My relationship with Wight was frosty even in those initial days. Pertaining to my frivolous fear that he would trick Brishen and I and turn us back to the platoon coupled with Wight's own personal apprehension. Brishen grumbled to me that we would be better off separating from our enigmatic leader, and while part of me agreed I felt we could not risk it; keep your enemies close, as they say. I wish now that I had listened to him. Furthermore, in Wight we had a thoughtful man who might procure some plan of action to our reckless desertion - a resolution, anything. Wight slowly warmed to us, albeit never truly relinquishing that bombastic sense of self-entitlment his former rank gave over us. The cries of war gave way to all the wild sounds of the mighty forest; for the better part of a fortnight we did wander betwixt those ancient pines, cutting our way in a northerly direction in hope that we might strike upon a suitable refuge. But we were a long way from safety, the three of us well aware of the dangers of wandering those Eastern states, concealed by forest or not. In my naivety, I had failed to inquire exactly why we headed northward, Brishen had entertained ideas of heading South in hopes of reaching the Mediterranean, whereby we may have stowed away on a seafaring vessel to greener pastures. But Wight had other ideas. He informed us of untouched villages in the tundra, of Siberia and Lapland, of an Ultima Thule[54] that I had only read of in stories. Therein lay townships enveloped in solitude, where we might steadily re-establish our livelihood - for better or worse, it did not matter - we were alive, we were away from that war, and that was all that counted. Our grizzled leader was better prepared for a long haul through the forests; I will admit Brishen and I looked foolishly meagre by comparison, for our packs were light and our supplies would not last much longer than a month or two. What we needed was money - something that might persuade the enemy to look the other way, something that might pardon us for a passage to our unseen destination, and an archaic keep we soon discovered in the Bohemian forest would provide a timely reassurance. Throughout our journey, we had seen numerous remnants of civilisations past; the forest had reclaimed many crumbled keeps and decayed townships, furnishing us with a keen feeling of isolation. Many of these locales had been ransacked long ago, so our delight in stumbling upon a more untouched keep was substantial. Within its ancient walls were humble treasures - water-logged chests of rusted coins and jewels dulled with grime; we had chanced on the vault of an old monarch, and whilst the rest of the structure had long since collapsed, these riches stood beckoning us with tempting coincidence. The three of us had little idea of their worth, but the one certain point was that it would be more than useful in our endeavours.

We remained at that keep for a week, and I wondered whether Wight had inadvertently decided that this would be the new home he had envisaged. To this he sneered, would these treasures fill our bellies? Could we continue living as amateur hunters in this unforgiving forest? No, he still had ambitions of travelling further north, and with these riches he had received a divine boon. But, said Brishen and I, did he not intend on splitting the treasures

---

[54] *Ultima Thule:* Often denoted as a far-northern locale beyond the borders of the known world.

equally, for it was all three of us that had discovered it? Wight would not look us in the eye, but made a less than convincing promise that yes, he would. Night came and we were thankful for a roof over our heads, for the rabbit we had caught and devoured, and for the first time since leaving England I felt a glimmer of hope kindled in my heart. It was a fleeting feeling; awaking in the small hours of night I espied a figure burdened with a heavy pack trudging uphill away from the castle. Knowing it to be Wight I flew to him and threw the traitor to the ground. In his shock, he cried out before begging me to quieten lest we awoke Brishen.

"And why should I not cut your throat right here, scoundrel?" said I, "You thought you could abandon us and take what is ours?"

Wight pushed me off of him and rose to his feet; standing above me on the inclined ground he looked imposing, in spite of his burden weighing heavily on his shoulders. In the heat of that moment I fail to recall the finer details of the ensuing conversation, in summary he told of his intent - he would continue on in his mission to seek salvation, and had I not appeared he would have gladly left us for dead in his wake. I cursed him for his utter lack of compassion to his fellow men, to which he replied had I not done the same in deserting the army? The trickster had a way with his words and I, a gullible fool, fell headlong into his snares. He gave me an ultimatum - I could follow him as his subordinate, he would ensure my life was spared and promised the same refuge he sought for himself. If I refused, he would kill me there. I felt a humourless laugh escape my mouth; Wight was an older man than I, and I had no doubt that I could overpower him physically. Eftsoons I cast my gaze to his hip, where the barrel of a pistol lay aimed directly at my heart. All at once that confidence left me, and I saw the calamity that had befallen me. I turned my head back to the keep entrance, where I knew Brishen still slept, oblivious. In hindsight I know I made the wrong decision. When torn between my own life and that of my friend I chose the selfish route. I would go with Wight. I would leave Brishen behind. That pivotal moment haunts even now, for it stood as the exact decision that placed me into Wight's tyrannical stranglehold, a hold that he would have on me for years to come and ultimately directed my life from there onward. Please, Vanesther, don't look that way. I know what this must look like, but there is more to tell.

****

According to the villagers the castle had always been there (although the integrity of their tale is shaky at best), and the abandoned Lapland keep gave off a certain longevous feel of centuries gone by. My guess had always been that some old Russian count must have lived there until he realised that the land held no value. But to Wight it was of value greater than gold. By now we had been travelling for months, stealing passage on the occasional freight train but mostly relying on our own two feet, and our wandering had led us to the forests Scandinavia. And so, despite the bad plumbing, hostile location and meek prospects, we began our new lives and for a while enjoyed the settled nature of such a quiet life. Yet this was no Valhalla, as with all new directions, I found the problems faced to be of an increasing concern. I of course stayed with Wight, agreeing with his notions under the illusion of youth and the fear of death; it would be too late for me to undergo a change of heart. Our treacherous cross-country trek had landed us here, and I shivered to think of the miles I would need to travel to recapture greater civilisation.

The villagers were feeble-minded idiots, yet malleable enough to be taught. Some would be happy to serve Wight, for they saw him as a white knight that had arrived with riches and technology to lead them into a new era. A few even went so far as to learn our language of English, minimal though the results may have been, it pleased Wight to have garnered such control. One villager stood out from amongst the rest like a florid bloom in a pile of dirt. Bianca was a bright young woman who seemed to cross the culture gap between us and the villagers faster than others. She carried a melancholic beauty in her frame, indeed she is still a wistful mystery for me to recall her now, and Wight would have her as his wife. The townsfolk were more than happy with this; for it brought them closer to the man they saw as saviour. Here Wight had achieved in establishing dominion over his fellow man; he could lead the life of prosperous solitude he had envisaged, where he could conceal the terrible treasures he had hoarded for himself."

XIX : The Man Once Known as Faron Silas

"And into my garden stole, When the night had veiled the pole; In the morning glad I see; My foe outstretched beneath the tree."

- William Blake

"Stop there, Faron. Brishen. My husband. You left him. You left my husband to die."

"Please Vanesther, I panicked as any youth would have. I saw my life ending prematurely right there, and bethought Brishen would have skills to survive alone."

"Fat lot of truth that turned out to be. Do you know how many years I've been left in the dark? How long I've yearned to know what happened to my husband - if he died a hero? Only to find it was his own friend who – who -" here she fought back sobs.

"It is a guilt I have lived with for decades. A guilt that has haunted me and ruined my life. I've lived in shadows ever since, the urge to force back the hands of the clock courses through my veins with such adrenalin. I did my friend the ultimate wrong, have I not suffered for it enough?"

"You should suffer twice over to atone for my own grief!"

There was little that Fairlie could say to console her; Vanesther stood slouched at the window, crippled with a rush of sorrow that had accumulated within her for decades. She had received her resolution - she knew what had befallen her husband. This knowledge coupled with the renewing of her old wounds was all at once too much to bear, and for several minutes neither she nor Fairlie spoke. She turned to face him, eyes bristling with a sudden fury with which she wished to strike down the instigator of her demise.

"I think you should leave."

Benumbed, Ereven Fairlie sat, as though he needed a moment to turn the command over in his head. Presently he stood, and as he gazed imploringly at Vanesther she no longer feared him as a ghost or as an antagonist, for she saw the glassy eyes of desperation plead for her pardon; she had the upper hand. Yet was this a look of true repentance or that of a man desperate to wheedle atonement for his own gain? He was not as she had remembered him; this was an old man, one who stood in the shadows of his former self.

"I will go," he said before procuring a tattered journal from his coat pocket, "I will leave this here for you. It may shed more light on my situation, but read it if you will."

"Don't leave your garbage here."

"Vanesther please, just think about it. If you read it and still have no wish to see me further, I will leave. This can just be some dream where I showed up briefly."

"If only."

Fairlie placed the journal down on the side table and left Vanesther standing alone in her loft. She moved immediately to the door and slammed down the lock then, feeling the relief of solitude, withdrew a cigarette and began to smoke. The journal lay ominously on the table, a horrible black obstruction to her racing thoughts. What game was he playing at? What could she possibly gain from reading the journal of a horrid old man? Yet the urge to leaf through its pages would not abate, for she wondered whether its story could reveal more about her husband, of whom she had finally been given a channel knowing toward his disappearance.

"To hell with it, I'll humour him." she muttered, seizing the journal and seating herself in her chair. As the wind began to howl outside she lit another cigarette and began to read.

****

By this point I was relying solely on Wight's bi-linguistics to communicate with others, and the loneliness that came with only having one other person to converse properly with slowly drove me to frustration. The miniscule utterances I had picked up from the odd villager had been enough for me to pass the time assisting in their farm work, a pastime undertaken purely to whittle away some of the agonising hours I had doomed myself to by following Wight to this place. I oft entertained the idea of bailing out once more and returning to England under a pseudonym; enough time had passed by now for me to make a fresh start. Money would be needed though, and Wight held our Bohemian treasures in such tight talons that I was left envying the stranglehold he had over me. And what payment could I expect from those dim-witted villagers? Their isolated community had but a primitive economy, one that would never advance me back in English society.

"You lack ambition," Wight would tell me, "had you the confidence to seize opportunity as I did, perhaps you would have amounted to these things you claim."

"I ask only for my own. There were three of us who discovered that bounty, and given the fate of Brishen I propose we split it evenly and go our separate ways."

Here Wight laughed, "Why I could never allow that! Well I guess you *would* think that. And I suppose you would spread news of your wartime heroics? Tell of the cowardly Walpole Wight who abandoned his post and left his men to defeat? Or mayhaps you'd tell of my clandestine domain here in these woods - and send the masses after me with malice and vengeance in their hearts?"

"Admit, man. We are nothing to one another. I would not gain anything by selling your reputation short."

"Ha! Yes, but therein lies the catch. You forget

that *I* spared *you!* It was I who gave you this life when I could have left you with that dunce, Brishen! It was *I* who gained nothing by having you tag along with me."

"Then you would condemn me to hell!"

"We are already in hell!" he barked, before calming once more, "Fact is that all the riches we discovered are right here in the castle. You may see them whenever you like. Why concern yourself with splitting our 'share' when that fact stands - your treasure is not going anywhere!"

To describe the fury I felt for him would be superfluous, suffice to say I was but a fly trapped in the web he had woven. Hindsight is a most bittersweet pill; would that I could turn back the pages of time and remain with Brishen - the friend I abandoned - I would undoubtedly do so. But I wanted riches. I admit I did the wrong thing; that one decision of mine had determined the fate of both of us. Brishen, forgive your foolish friend.

****

Our scant population is rapidly dwindling. They cry about becoming curse-stricken, however I feel there must be some sort of poison in the water. Villagers of all ages are taken ill by a violent fever and expire within a few days. It is a truly horrific sight to observe such a savage malady, coupled with such a precipitous decline into death; those I could speak to in good health one day are on death's road the next. I am unsure whether or not Wight has something to do with it all. The estate's residents show no signs of the awful illness - whether this is due to the quarantine nature of our lodgings, of our cleanlier livings, again I do not know. Some have hinted towards Wight's 'dealings with the devil'; our ever-suspicious town fearing a divine wrath has been brought upon them from some misdeed governed by Wight.

Bianca's health is of concern though; she does not

show signs of fever at all yet appears weak with worry over her husband, and no doubt my presence only makes the situation more strenuous. Perhaps I should fear this journal falling beneath the wrong eyes - Wight is so insufferably paranoid he would discover how those around him actually feel. How ironic that he himself would descend into paranoia after laughing at those gullible and easily manipulated villagers. I've said that none could best his wit - perhaps he fears a mutiny by those closest to him; myself and Bianca his chief suspects. I want to leave. I *will* leave, one way or another. Bianca should join me. It is not good for a young woman's health to dwell in this damp castle with such miserable company. Her sheltered upbringing means she has the naivety of a child, yet she is undoubtedly intelligent enough. My fondness for her company is lurching dangerously towards infidelity. How can I ignore my heart? Ignore the chance for affection after years of horrible isolation, of disconnection? Be it a scapegoat or not, I feel she shares this fondness; alas the heart truly is deceitful above all things, desperately wicked; who indeed can know it?

****

I am dancing with the devil now. I know it. *Danse Macabre*, was it? My traitorous heart has set itself on her. I would be a fool to act upon these feelings. More foolish still to write any more on the matter.

****

It is not as I thought. Bianca has not taken ill, but is with child. It cannot be mine. Surely not. Were it true, I might as well burn *myself* at the stake and save Wight the bother. He has reason to believe she carries twins, and it chills me to think of that dreary offspring, damned at conception.

****

Wept for the man today. I don't know why. A deep sorrow filled my heart to tipping point; perhaps I ponder too much on what could have been. And when on the precipice of penance, what man doesn't think of how fate could have been altered? It shouldn't have been this way, stuck in this purgatory of pines; what good are the treasures we found when we sleep amongst peasants in the wilderness? Useless! Dangle a bloody pinecone in front of those villagers and you could convince them it's holy. Does Wight get some sort of power trip from this? Surely he has stooped well below his own standards. The man commanded a platoon and now would prefer to manipulate these townsfolk who've the minds of babes. Well I don't want this anymore. I write 'anymore' as if I wanted it in the first place. Damn this forgotten corner of the world, I want my share; I want to return to England.

They fear him like a god or daemon, and so too does his unfortunate pregnant wife. Although it had never been what one might call a happy union, still Bianca fears for her husband and grows fearful of his dwindling sanity. His days are increasingly spent in isolation, locked in his study where even Bianca is forbidden to enter. A change in the man's demeanour is obvious - a heightened paranoia - our brief conversations are riddled with scorn and accusations of treachery. I fear he may already be aware of my debauchery, of his wife's unfaithfulness, and feels that I intend to steal everything off of him.

****

I have been banished from the castle.

****

Twin girls. Beautiful things, ethereal as the moon's umbra.

What would become of these stunning creatures? Bianca is naturally attuned to motherhood. The love she has for these girls equalled the fear she has of her husband, yet the light of this love is the only brightness to shine in this dark age of which we dwell. The three of them are of ill health, however. I fear the newborns may not survive these harsh conditions, particularly with their mother in such poor physical health (noble though her intentions may be).

****

Wight is not a well man. His inclusiveness steadily grows - there are times now where several days may pass without us conversing. I suppose I should not complain, but I was wary of what he was doing in that wing of the castle. What horrible plot was he following? Since my banishment from the castle, there would be no way I could enter those chambers unannounced without repercussion; I had to be discreet. For Bianca's sake I had to know what he was up to. She weeps for her absent husband - poor creature - cursed with that residue of melancholy that cloaks the villagers of this land, and I can offer little to comfort her. So, during a rare moment of recreation on Wight's part - namely a short stroll about the grounds of his forsaken home - I took it upon myself to interrogate that clandestine portion of the estate and see for myself what ploy, if any, my old adversary was up to.

Compelled by rebellion my feet did clamber up the stairs to that isolated wing. I felt that nervous trepidation that comes with being in a place that one is not meant to tread; wandering through the cave of a sleeping bear and praying the beast does not notice. Sweat clung to my skin in spite of the loveless cold that echoed in the castle. A large wooden door withheld the secrets of Wight's demise; the fool had left it unlocked, perhaps he wasn't quite as paranoid as I had thought. Perhaps, more likely, he had instilled enough fear into those closest to him that he felt no need to. Indeed the wing was far enough away from the living quarters, and this was *his* home - we were just underlings living in it. We knew the consequences of stepping out of line. In any account, the door groaned loudly on its hinge; I hissed a curse of excruciating anguish through my teeth and paused for a moment to drink of the silence that followed. Mercifully, no-one had heard me open the door. I entered. Instantly I would notice the smell. An awful, cloying odour sticky with the pungency of death. That acrid scent brought with it the terrifying memories of men rotting in a field after those battles in Bohemia. The air was heavy with it, cold rot and blood was unmistakably present even with the burning incense, much like a hospital ward that tries and fails to hide the inevitability of its purpose. The room was large but poorly ventilated, choked with dust and clutter and lit dimly by window slits cut high up into the stone facade. Candles, many that had been recently extinguished, sat all around the room, ribbons of smoke trailing up from their wicks and billowing into a gentle cloud above. Clearly Wight had been using the space as some sort of laboratory, for books lay piled all about with any number of scientific utensils and equipment. And further amongst that stench (Gods, that horrible stench), the room held the qualities of a hoarder's vault. For I saw any great number of the wonderful treasures we had ransacked from those Bohemian keeps. It would be with a twitch of jealousy mingled with remorse that I observed those trinkets, their sheen dulled by the years of neglect, their lustre blunted by coatings of dust and damp. Jealousy, because Wight had used his sense of authority (a sleight of hand more than anything) to lay claim to those treasures. Remorse, due to the lack initiative I had shown at the time to claim what was *my* share. Perhaps I had held a lingering respect for the man who had spared me the wrath of the army and offered me this acceptable if not meagre life. What use were those riches to anybody? What mirth had they bestowed upon my bitter old colleague? I pondered the worth that man put on earthly possessions and cursed myself for following that same squandered path. For though I knew myself to be no better than the next man, still I craved those siren songs, those fruits of the tree. I cursed myself because I knew there was no use in coveting those mildewed riches; for there I was, a thief in the night, ready to strike and steal what was perhaps Wight's most precious treasure.

My thoughts, foolishly diverting me from my purpose, stuttered to an interrupted halt at the presence of a sound, a sound that froze my heart with such fear I fancied the blood pounding in my temples might burst from my ears. A grunt, was it? A scratching of a branch against the castle wall? Surely it had been a muttering of the wind or hiss of the rustling autumn leaves. A frantic survey of the room confirmed my isolation, though I still could not shake the sensation of being watched; the few candles that remained alight had eyes, their guttering flames offering no solace but rather piercing me with the loveless gaze of men gone mad. Their light threw shadows about the room, illuminating the massive table that choked the large space and made it feel more cramped than it was. It was the contents of this table that would arrest my gaze, for there lay scattered dust-clotted parchments displaying wicked symbology of pentagrams[55] and ram's heads, interspersed with scribblings of a language I did not recognise. The cold imagery of it all sent further chills down my spine, as I gasped in horror at the paper weight Wight had been using for these documents - a skull that was undeniably human. The eyes of my nemesis, seen all over these documents through 'eye-of-providence' relics and sketches of constellations, led me to believe that Wight was in fact watching me at that very moment. With much effort, I looked away from those horrible notes, only

---

[55] *Pentagram:* A five-pointed star often seen as a symbol of the occult.

to have my senses inundated with the pungent odours that had preoccupied me earlier. My heart sank further to espy a small change speckled about the stone floor, markings that could not escape my view once I had noticed them. A tonal quality, one that broke the monochromatic decor and filled me with a dread much more potent than before, a horrible *dark red* stained the floor in splotches that could only be blood. Stricken, I quivered at the knees and had to fight to remain standing, for I felt a swoon overcome me and threaten to send me floor bound onto those sickly stains. But what (or dare I say *who*) could this blood have come from?

I realised then that the room extended much further than I'd originally been able to calculate, cut off by towering book shelves and heavy black curtains. Did I dare venture further into this tortuous lair of the enemy? Better for Daniel to enter the den of lions[56] than for me to be where I was at that moment, however I had come too far to back away now. Were it tangible, I believed the wicked stench to increase on the drawing of that dark tapestry, and with horror I saw at once the source of those deathly scents. For it was indeed death that clouded the air; there all at once invading my senses, were several barrels filled with the severed limbs and trunks of cadavers, some decayed heads of once human beings held fast in paralysed anguish with death's head grimace. How I held my resolve at this stage, I cannot say, but to recall the terrifying scene brings the tears flowing back, the gorge to the tip of my throat, and my brain seems to do all it can to repress the horror. For these were not the humane specimens of a qualified physician, no - these were villagers from the township below the castle! Alas I struggle to describe the things I saw; men, women - and to my dismay, children - all murdered by the hands of Wight, hacked to pieces for whatever evil occult he had been practising. When I felt

---

[56] *Better for Daniel to enter the den of lions...:* Daniel 6:1–28.

my senses could not bear another magnitudinous shock, that groaning I had heard earlier returned, louder, and I felt a wet warmth clutch my ankle meekly. Turning my gaze downward ever slowly, fearing what I would see, there upturned the face of a dolorous humanoid; what was once a man now lay sprawled and naked, barely alive and clutching at my ankle with a bloodstained hand. Here I shrieked with a most potent fear I never thought possible to imagine, and the near-dead corpse man cried weakly in reply, his milky eyes pleading with me for mercy, to stamp out his existence and end his suffering. I fell backwards onto my haunches and realised then that no, I had not been alone in this room, not by a long shot. Besides that crawling chaos that had grabbed at me, on the walls at the back of this room hung more of these mutilated corpses - many of them somehow alive, their flames of life all but ailing flickers; had I stumbled upon the ninth circle[57]? Never had I thought such suffering could be endured in this world, and later I would wonder just how long those condemned humanoids would cling to life before clemency would snuff them from this world. Their eyes cried for a saviour and I, coward that I am, turned about face and ran for the door. I could handle no more, and knew I could share this with no-one, for I would be no better than Wight were I to fill another mind with the imagery of what I'd seen. I would have to burden the brunt of the trauma, trauma that still sends shivers down my spine to this day; burden the guilt that came from doing little to rescue any that might have survived Wight's tortures.

****

---

[57] *Ninth circle:* The Divine Comedy (written 1308–1320) the last and innermost of nine localities in Dante Aligheiri's depiction of Hell.

Won't write much on this. Going to leave. It needs to happen now. She'll come with me. Perhaps the girls must come with us? Impossible. Call me heartless but we cannot afford to be slowed up in any way; no, I am not heartless. It is only that my heart belongs entirely to her and her alone. Wight would not hurt his family, this much I know; not that such a fact would ever justify his actions. Those poor babes, of whom neither parent could claim to be adequate. We will leave them with the villagers. I know it will not be long until Wight reclaims them both but I do not dare shatter Bianca's lingered hope. The hour draws near.

XX : The Forest for the Trees

"Abashed the devil stood and felt how awful goodness is…"

- John Milton

The Parisian sky was pregnant with clouds that threatened to burst a deluge on the streets. Wind gusts that would precede the rain carried mystery on their breath - mysteries of burning betrayal, of secrets kept too long, so that even the wind could not hold them any longer. Like mourners at the Wailing Wall certain truths yearned to be wrung dry from the clandestine cloak of the arcane. The wisp of the candle flame caught hold of this cloak; flames that would not be obscured burned hotly with decades of resentment.

None will know the hour or the day.[58]

The coffee had gone cold before Vanesther, and as she gazed vacantly at a certain linden leaf whirling about the street her cigarette was almost out, with nothing left to burn in its three-inch stick of ash. Conjointly the secrets that were coming to a head would not have much more left to burn, but there still remained enough fuel to scar those it threatened. With her other hand she turned Fairlie's journal slowly. Was that all there was? The tale betwixt its pages had ended so abruptly. *It had to be some part of his plot*, Vanesther had thought, *a cliff-hanger that would grab my attention*. Yet he had succeeded, for there she sat, having agreed to meet him in a neutral venue, wherein she might obtain further clarification for what the journal had so tantalisingly teased. Yes, none would know the hour or the day, but one could assume the hour was nigh. While

---

[58] *None will know the hour or the day:* paraphrasing of Matthew 25:13.

the baristas were busy battening down their awnings in the
ensuing storm, the bell above the entrance chimed and
Ereven Fairlie appeared before Vanesther once more. His
physique was somehow more ghostly in the grey daylight,
for only under the brighter light could she properly
perceive the scars of age carved ruthlessly on his face, and
his emaciated frame was swallowed in the dusty
monochrome of his coat. He approached with that same
pitiful expression - a beaten dog, or a reprimanded child.
Though he stood over her table he asserted no dominance,
and Vanesther in her powerfully lax countenance brushed
her hand as an invitation to sit down. Fairlie did so and
remained silent for a moment; courtesy had not been
native to his personality, and as such his silence brought
frustration to Vanesther rather than his intention of
allowing her to speak first.

Vanesther clearly would not have a bar of it. She had
humoured this treacherous apparition and, although many
lingering questions remained surrounding her husband,
had little wish to speak with him. She sighed impatiently
and wordlessly urged the man to *spit it out already, whatever it
is you have to say!*

"Thank you for meeting with me,"
Thank you? Well that's a nice generic civility.

"I- I gather you may have more questions to ask."

Vanesther crushed her cigarette into the ashtray and
lit another, exhaling smoke with careless abandon, "What
more can you tell me? I know my husband is dead because
of you; I know my life is the way it is because of you."

"Ness, I have apologised. I would apologise a
thousand times…"

"Do not call me that," she interrupted, "I heard you
out, and you shook my life to pieces for a second time.
Would you kindly leave me be? Or would you spoil my
existence further?"

"Vanesther; I have reason to be here, I assure you."
Fairlie shuffled in his seat and leaned towards her, "I

informed you of that wicked man, Walpole Wight…"

"Pot. Kettle. Black."

"I recently received news that he has died, *and left his riches to me*. The riches I once laid claim to."

Vanesther twisted her face in irritated bemusement, "Well good for you, you miserable old miser. More money for you - why drag me into it?"

"Point is," Fairlie patiently replied, "For reasons I will not bore you with, I need to remain scarce for a while. I've lived a miserable existence in London, lavish though it may appear. I've all the makings of a wealthy home but no friends to share it with."

"Faron, you're making no sense. Why should I care for your plight? What stops me from throwing you to whatever wolves chase you - like you did with Brishen?"

"Because, Vanesther," here he sighed, "*I don't think that Walpole Wight is dead.* I believe he is very much alive, and he is coming for me."

Fairlie paused, hoping for empathy from his potential saviour, but Vanesther maintained her steely glare.

"There is no way he would leave me a cent. It sensed suspicion the moment I received the letter informing me of his passing. I ignored the summons that would have me revisit his estate, for I feared it to be a trap. He would kill me, had he the chance, I know it. How he uncovered my changed identity, I've no idea. Please Vanesther, he will search for me in England, and I've nowhere else to hide. I beg of you that I may lay low here."

"What makes you think he will actively search for you?"

"You read of my plans to elope with Bianca, his young wife," he paused momentarily, "Fact is when we had tried to escape Wight's clutches - Bianca was killed."

Vanesther listened with an increased intensity. He could certainly spin a tale; what fresh allegations would arise from this unseen muse?

"During our escape she fell through the ice of the

nearby lake - she drowned."

So it's the star-crossed lost lover spiel, I never was one for doomed romance.

"You may no doubt wonder," Fairlie continued, "how many more twists this tale may have."

"You should write a script." Vanesther sneered.

"I'll leave that one to you artistic types. But suffice to say it is Bianca's death that harbours the most resentment in Wight. He holds me responsible, and although I can't blame him for that, he does not see that it was he who drove her to me."

Fairlie checked himself, for he was becoming flustered and did not want to betray any evil intent towards his only salvation.

"So you're here to ask an accessory of me? In exchange for the promise of 'riches'? Sounds a little familiar to me." Here she shook the journal towards him.

She took great enjoyment in watching his shoulders slumped with defeat; like a cat that toys with a mouse before killing it she held him on tenterhooks, and she used his prolonged anticipation to carefully come to a decision of her own. Did she dare allow herself to become further involved in this madness? The waiter approached and informed them in a false politeness that the cafe would be closing soon on account of the incoming storm. A look of bleak desperation came across the face of Ereven Fairlie - he saw his one chance rapidly evaporating before his eyes. As Vanesther stood, the first clap of thunder roared on the street outside, and the wind quickened to a gale. Were Fairlie a more fanciful man he'd have attributed the woman towering before him as the bringer of said lightning.

With a voice as rough as sand Vanesther spoke, "You gave me a resolution of sorts regarding my dear Brishen. I suppose I should thank you for that. But it does little to atone for what you've done to me."

She strode purposefully to the door of the cafe and

paused, looking over her shoulder at the beaten man still seated behind her.

"Well," she said, "Come on then. Before I change my mind."

XXI : The Madman's Note

"For the Panic of the Wilderness had called to him in that far voice – the Power of untamed Distance – the Enticement of the Desolation that destroys."

- Algernon Blackwood

"I never wanted to fight. When I was a boy I wanted to be a clergyman. The old man hated me for it. Said the church wasn't relevant in these modern times. The prick is probably burning now. Serves him right. Thought I could be a poet. Thought joining the war would be romantic, would give me the worldly experience needed to write. Idiot. Too many war stories growing up. They painted it as an heroic jubilee. Why did I ever think I'd be like Beowulf[59]? Like Taras Bulba[60]? Napoleon? I hate Napoleon. Fuck the guy. I want to go home."

"The Cossacks are far more savage than I'd ever imagined."

"Faron and the other bloke have gone. Fucking bastards left me behind. Woke up this morning alone. The loot was gone too, no doubt the cowards wanted to leave me for dead. Wonder if the two of them have cut each other's throats yet."

"I never should have gone with them. I could have shot them both dead and gone back to the platoon. Hell,

---

[59] *Beowulf:* (700–1000 A.D.? by unknown author) Titular hero of the Old English epic poem of the same name. Beowulf was brought to fame and glory after slaying several beasts threatening various Norse lands.

[60] *Taras Bulba:* Ukrainian Cossack and war hero. Protagonist of Nikolai Gogol's 1835 novella of the same name.

they'd have done me the same favour - dare I say they've already assigned me to such a fate by abandoning me. They were nothing to me; I thought I could just get my hands on some of that bounty, and then I'd be set. I am a fool. But Faron - how could you do this to me? I thought we were friends."

"My supplies are dwindling. The pack grows lighter every day - a blessing perhaps? Or rather a sickening reminder of my impending fate. I need to find someone, anyone soon or it's curtains. They'd brandish me with cowardice; I'd probably be punished, but that is small compared to the alternative, wandering aimlessly to my demise in this forest."

"Ness, good God I miss her. I fear I won't see her again. The very thought sinks my gut into a void. I envisage myself on sinking sand, the waters around me savage and unconquerable."

"The trees have eyes. Those lights; every night they return. They watch me like I'm some puppet in a show."

"No idea what day it is. Forgot to record one day and now I'm just confused. It's hot so I assume we're still in summer. Sweating so much and water seems to be eluding me. I believe my ears to be hearing a creek somewhere but my skills are failing me. What is wrong with me? My mind is so foggy. I've never felt this before."

"Cut my leg today. Feel like a damn fool. Saw that bloody tree branch a mile away and still slammed straight into it. Christ the blood wouldn't stop. Had little choice but to tourniquet it with some of my clothing. But now I am more exposed to the elements, and walking is troublesome. Damn it all."

"I'm burning under this sun. The pain is so itchy. My skin weeps and cracks."

"All of the pieces are still there; they just don't fit together anymore. But please Ness, even in the thickest fog remember that I love you and that has not changed."

"I won't make it. I can't stay here. I am afraid."

"Thinking of the horrible things I've seen makes me sick. If I could only forget; my mind is being selective. I am having trouble remembering most things these days."

"Bird flew here. Spoke to bird. Bird flew away. I cried out for bird but bird didn't come back so I cried."

"Bird flew here."

"Cried."

"The sun hurts so much. Prayers for rain."

"Saw a flame and followed. Follow flame to trees. So many trees. So many fire."

"Lights chasing. Fire chasing. Darkness coming."

"Walking a lot. Feet hurt. Sun is hot so thirsty. Fire. Trees make me slow. Fire. Help me. I need help."

"D...r...knes... com...n...g."

(unintelligible)

XXII : Revelations

"It's you who are telling me; opening my eyes to things I'd looked at so long that I'd ceased to see them."

-   Edith Wharton

After navigating the bustling London streets for the first time, Hemlocke Wight could be excused for breathing a sigh of relief as she and her camaraderie entered the echoing halls of Fairlie's mansion. To her, the bright lights of a major city had been a myth hitherto, however her reaction to such a crude shock was rather muted considering. For this reason alone, Pinnacle Tricks found it odd that the young woman appeared more irritable than ever and, unlike her sister Ague (who had been dumbstruck by the city lanterns like a moth to flame), she had grown increasingly nervous as their long journey had gone on. Perhaps her anxiety was attributed to the uncertainty of her future; the mention of her father was always met with a submissive reverence that told of an overtly controlling patron. As for Tricks, although the job was not quite finished yet, he felt the weight of his burden lighten; his pilgrimage was surely reaching its conclusion - soon he could return to his beloved wife. He had already rehearsed a resignation letter in his mind, and it was to his great frustration that Fairlie had not been home to receive it.

Typical of him! Trick roared internally, *Will I ever escape this awful station?*

He wished he had seen the light earlier; the wasted months he had spent aimlessly wandering Europe left a bitter taste in his mouth. Despite the experiences it afforded, and the enviable gaiety of the wanderer, he realised that his time was much better spent with his family. Yes, work was important, but his loved ones could not be compromised.

Their party had once again dwindled to a trio. Cedrus and his crew had left them at the harbour where the old captain had claimed they would remain for a week or so before shipping back to Reykjavik. Pinnacle and Ague agreed that they would miss young Oddbergur, while Hemlocke seemed more concerned with ensuring their luggage was not lost or tampered with. Her paranoia was no doubt attributed to the sheltered life she had lived; her belongings had always been in that same house in the Lapland forest, where she knew her own version of the truth to be, although now her old life seemed so distant that she doubted its tangibility at all. Unbeknownst to Pinnacle, Hemlocke awaited the next moments on bated breath; she had been forced into thinking quickly after Fairlie had failed to appear at Wight Estate, instead sending Pinnacle. It had sent everything into chaos, and she groped desperately to bring things back to a calm. It was therefore little wonder that she too shared the frustrations of Tricks when they were informed that Mr. Ereven Fairlie had left his home days ago, with no indication of when he might return. When the elderly butler had opened the mighty oak doors of the house she was certain - yes, this must be the man she was after. But no, the little man had announced himself as one Atlas Egerton, chief servant of Mr. Fairlie. *Servant*, indeed! She hated the man she had never met even more. But soon it would matter not. Hemlocke knew her moment was near.

Atlas Egerton had welcomed the returning Tricks

with the fondness of an old friend, although they had only ever been mere acquaintances. Tricks himself commented that he had never ventured further beyond the foyer of his superior's great home, and when he, Ague and Hemlocke were escorted to the chief drawing room of the estate Pinnacle swore through his teeth at the opulence his master possessed. Why had he even bothered with this whole Wight ordeal? Clearly the old miser did not need more riches. And to send him on the errand instead! It was enough to further enrage young Tricks. Meanwhile Atlas shuffled this way and that, unsure of what to do with the strange visitors in his master's absence. He could not turn the girls away after such a journey, but what of Fairlie's undeniable disdain for the girls' deceased father? Did they know of their father's feud with the man whose house they now stood within? By now the sun had set, the other servants had gone home, and the house thundered with echoes, cloaked itself with shadows and an air of suspense pervaded on an encroaching storm. Atlas scurried about the kitchen, the cellars, the many spare bedrooms.

Should a meal be prepared? The guest rooms readied? But how long would they be staying? To bring refreshments? Wine? No! Now was not time to celebrate, these girls are still mourning!

Through the gusty corridors Atlas heard a familiar thud - the sound of the oak front doors slamming shut. The cold metal clash of the bolt locking followed immediately.

Odd, he thought, *but there are other issues to attend.*

At last he realised how to make himself most useful. For while he had been shuffled about the house this way and that, his visitors had been sitting in that cold drawing room without a fire. The light had dimmed when he returned, the day entering that strange transition between twilight and evening; he found the trio sitting silently on the antiquated sofa chairs. Giving them little attention, Altas moved straight to the task at hand, snatching the bellows and conjuring up a flame with expert marksmanship.

"Quiet lot, you all are," he chuckled, and the lack of immediate response made him uneasy.

Again came the sound of a door locking - this time closer than before, in fact Atlas could have sworn, without turning his head, that someone had just locked them in the drawing room. A voice cut through savagely the gloom, and Atlas felt his heart lurch with fear. The heat of the fire, the coldness of the room, the sweat in his armpits - all became instinctually clear - *the voice was not one that he recognised.*

"Stand up."

The butler heard the cock of a loaded gun. He turned slowly on his feet, arms aloft in submission. At first he could not see clearly, for the light of the fire had left his eyes unaccustomed to the darkness of the room. He could discern Wight's daughters on the sofa, their enigmatic expressions not unlike the drama and comedy masks Atlas had seen at the theatre. The face of Ague - vacant, insane, sickeningly cheerful; Hemlocke - her face was one of admitted guilt and betrayal. Pinnacle Tricks sat paralysed, and Atlas saw another man standing behind Tricks – a man who was the owner of the voice. Against the night-lit window panes, now rain-streaked with the arrival of a storm, the ghostly figure stood ominously. The shock of his white hair and rheumy eyes gave him the appearance of a demon risen from the grave, and Atlas saw the glistening barrel of the pistol aimed squarely before the figure.

His voice was gravelly and slow, "Where is the man who owns this house?"

Atlas felt his knees shake, the piss streamed down his leg and he whimpered at the indignity. He could barely respond, so intense was his fear, "W-we don't know... B-but who are you?"

The horrifying man smirked, his face a death's head grimace, "I am Wight. Walpole Wight."

XXIII : Doctor Flatwoods' Account
Scottish Highlands, 1889

"But alas! My Lord, what is blood! What is nobility! We are reptiles, miserable, sinful creatures. It is piety alone that can distinguish us from the dust whence we sprung, and whither we must return."

- Horace Walpole

Of all the patients held beneath my Hippocratic wing, none have impressed their lunacy upon my heart quite like the Old Skallywag. An otherwise anonymous vagabond brought portentously into my care through what my fanciful side would label as an act of divinity. To recall that night some three decades ago - *Has it been that long?* - is to bring forth those feelings one might entertain in visiting memories of pivotal consequences - perhaps a reaction to hearing of a death in the family, or news that rattles life's normalcy inasmuch as to become tattooed into the mind - permanent and unforgettable. A lifetime spent in the field of medicine has left me somewhat jaded, as all careers are wont to do, yet my visits to Inveraray Gaol always brought with them a particular dread; perhaps in part to the dreary travel necessary from Glasgow to the bay, past Loch Lomond and its misty shores, into the Highlands where mystery seems to lurk in the dampness. Indeed, nothing leaves me quite so crestfallen as that journey into 'the storm' as I'll call it, even though a Scot should perhaps be used to such weather, and arriving in town to see that awful establishment perched across the water like an ugly vulture, ready to pick at whatever shreds of passion might still flicker in my benumbed countenance.

I have never been a prison guard, nor has the Old Skallywag ever been a true prisoner (a prisoner of the mind, perhaps, but that may be getting too whimsical for my liking). Yet the fates would have it that our paths cross at that dreary penitentiary, where my suspicions of his being a unique case were sparked by an unfortunate incident involving his incarceration. Often I would find myself called out at obscene hours to respond to urgent maladies but still the night that I received a call from the warden at Inveraray[61] carried with it a peculiar dread, for his voice shook with uncertainty, and spoke of a most unusual gentleman to be admitted to his cellblock. I arrived at the gaol just past the witching hour, during that hazy time before dawn where life feels but a dream and reality can't find anchor in yesterday or tomorrow. Rain fell comfortless on the shoulders of the warden, waiting outside to greet me as though he feared that which had fallen into his care. I had known this man many years - *seen* the iron fist unto which his prisoners struggled; never had I espied that sort of reservation in him hitherto. And I would *hear* his reasons why before I saw them; the prison walls echoed with an inhuman wailing, sick with the night and storm. Inhuman, indeed would be the apt tie to his appearance as well - an emaciated figure, limbs brittle and malnourished, ribs stretching tight the skin of his torso, body hairless but for the shock of white hair atop his crown.

Stricken, I gathered the strength scattered by that initial visage, and I remember the guard standing cautiously behind me, as though my own limp and fleshy frame might shield him from the beast.

"Couldn't get much from the authorities on this one,"

---

[61] *Inveraray:* Gaol in the Scottish Highlands operating 1820–1889.

he said, "whole thing stinks of conspiracy."

"Well I wouldn't go so far as that, but this man clearly belongs in a hospital."

"Wouldn't take him."

"Aye," said I, "perhaps the man would feel better with some clothing?"

The prisoner resisted our best attempts to clothe him; he seemed to prefer pressing his skull to the bars of the window and let the rain wet his face. He thrashed in our arms, causing him to strike his head against the wall several times, until his forehead was bloody and bruised. Did he cry with pain? No - reader, I tell you, he laughed each time he was struck, and took on a vampiric grin as the blood trickled from his fresh wounds. Self-flagellation is unfortunately common in the patients I treat, but never had I seen such reckless disregard for one's own well-being. He was seemingly numb to the pain, or at least derived sensations from it other than pain. Still, despite the struggles, we would eventually soothe him, and the warden could brief me on what he knew. Found naked and raving in the Bohemian forest, the man in question belied himself as English through his derelict utterances. He was assumed to be a soldier from the war in Crimea. In spite of his obvious civilities (albeit now lost), none appeared to claim him. No platoon held record of missing men to the extent of his situation; naked as he was found meant that nothing could differentiate him from any other nameless soldier perished in battle. There was little anybody could do for him, and the man was clearly in no state to reside in regular society. How shamefully our society treats the impaired.

I could not help but commiserate with the man, who over time, despite his appearing several years older than myself, became not unlike an unfortunate younger brother. I prayed for him, prayed that some bezoar existed that could relieve his malady, but such fruitless thought would have been of little benefit to anybody. Blood poisoned with madness, a brain decayed before its time, I named him the Old Skallywag, for he could give no other name for himself. To him, I was the only one with whom he would speak respectfully, and I took great pride in being as helpful as any could be to the poor man's plight.

If his sudden arrival had not been bizarre enough, his crazed demeanour contained further oddities which I discovered only through the years which followed. Seemingly, he did not age - that haggard face remained unchanged as though the world around him froze as his mind slipped from its perch. His face had an elastic quality to it, as though it could be pressed into any given gargoyle shape. Carrying himself with the lumbering stature of a tall man he was somewhat short; this contradictory posture lending to his appearance familiarities with the works of De Goya[62]. In many ways he inspired the image of a monochromatic fire; his hair twisted itself in bedraggled tangles laced with black turned to grey. Then there were the behavioural oddities which lent to many a puzzling thought as I journeyed to and fro the Highlands on my frequent visits. Like many debilitated by trauma he loved routine, and perhaps the indifferent walls of his prison provided him with but a minor form of contentedness in an otherwise strange world he had found himself in. Any swaying from regularity would send him into a frenzy, and those that tended to him had to ensure they remained prompt to the minute to keep a famous temper from exploding.

The weather held him under a peculiar hypnotism (I am reminded of the old quacks and their term 'lunatic' - driven to madness by the moon). On days where the wind and rain would howl he would expose himself to the small patch of flagstone beneath his solitary window, allowing

---

[62] *The works of De Goya:* Francisco De Goya (1746–1828). Spanish artist whose paintings and etchings often depicted demoniac and grotesque imagery.

the rain to spit its drops at him without the least concern for his inconvenience. Dramatising his hallucinations with grotesque realism, he hated fire and held the sunlight with discontent. So much that he would pace his cell anxiously, careful to avoid the barred square of light shining in. He rattled his chains like a dog on a leash, until his ankle was stripped to its bone, and the emaciated flesh hung in red ribbons around the irons. Stricken man! Scattered unfortunate!

The obscenities he would bark! Such foul language he could spew to make me cross myself, for even the most hardened Judas would weep to hear such horrific profanity. Truly he was an enigma; littered amongst his ramblings were snippets of beautiful poetry - be they his own or some other's that he had memorised I do not know - and the scriptures he would oft quote could make my own bosom swell with melancholy. Poor man! Yet one felt the Lord wrestle with the enemy for his attention. Could there be comfort drawn from the knowledge of our good Lord's grace - despite this man's obvious demons? I could only hope. He would oft cry for his muse; some woman he swore he would 'fly home to', and betwixt his wretched sobs one could discern his longing for 'his nest'. I assumed his imaginary siren to be a 'Vanessa' or sometimes 'Esther', although his cries were always so grief-stricken as to leave his words less than coherent. It made me ponder his former life; had he a wife? (No doubt she would assume herself a widow and, given his condition, she might as well have been). Children? Those poor offspring robbed of their patron figure. What of interests, of hobbies? What had life held for this man had Bonaparte not marched East? What dreams were dashed?

****

For years I championed attempts to have him transferred to a proper asylum where he could be monitored with greater care and attention. The new hospital at Hartwood[63] would be the perfect tonic; closer to Glasgow and better fitted to handle a man of his case. I have been his attendant for years. Why do I write of him now? Let it be known that at present, I fear for him. His fits worsen; my gravest concern is that he will be whipped of his life by the prison guards before he can be transported to the asylum. He does not belong here. Although he seems to be untroubled or oblivious to the taunts of the inmates it is obvious to me that they mock him.

This afternoon I visited the Old Skallywag and found him to be in a state of quiet contentedness. We sat vis-a-vis; he upon the matted straw of his bed and I on the cheerless ground. It would be the first time I had sat so leisurely in the presence of a patient, and were it not for our attire betraying our individual stations, an outsider would consider us two good friends sharing a yarn.

"Halloween comes early this year, doctor," he said quite surely, "The black gale howls through the minds of the dryads - one is mad, the other is sad!"

"Is that so?" responded I (for who could glean anything from such nonsense?)

"Oh Melmoth[64], wandering Jew[65]! Melmoth is here! Cowards - they all return from where they fled."

His gaze was unsettling; again that elasticity had twisted the face into a cold horror, and it was this gaze that seemed to stare directly through me. How chilling becomes the calm smile of a madman! How unsettling the

---

[63] *Hartwood:* Psychiatric hospital in outer Glasgow opened in 1895.

[64] *Melmoth:* Melmoth The Wanderer was a Gothic novel by Charles Robert Maturin. The titular character would appear before suffering people and attempt to barter their salvation for his curse.

[65] *Wandering Jew:* Maturin's work was inspired by the tale of the Wandering Jew – a man cursed to walk the earth for all eternity after mocking the crucified Christ.

shudders he evokes with lies hidden behind charlatan pleasantries! Controlling me with the ease of a lion with its cornered prey did those horrible oculi. Freeing me from his gaze he moved to the window of his cell he stated quite simply, "I think it's going to rain."

Eftsoons he turned his face to me again and said, "I could be wrong."

He had not eaten for some time but when I queried him he professed that he hungered not.

"Dost thou think the spider cannot see the fly? She has eight eyes! Eight - they see all. Her stillness is but a facade! She strikes! Death befalls those who feel the sting of her poison."

Here he cackled horribly. The lightning struck, and the fool in me shuddered that perhaps this man had control over those elements. Lord forgive the fear in my heart! The cloying scent of his putrid cell was enough to make me swoon, and only my many years of experience in this profession were able to bring me to composure. I felt the need to somehow swing his thoughts towards those of optimism and thought to inquire about his favourite poets, for it was obvious that he held the medium in high regard. He looked at me, his face painted with a death's head grimace, *risus sardonicus*[66].

"Some burns never heal, doctor," he whispered, "*these* burns will never heal. *The wisp*, the scars may fade, but the burns never heal."

It soon came time for me to leave; having encouraged him to sup on something, anything for strength, he nodded his head mournfully and again looked out the window. Thinking him to be in a reasonable state of calm I moved towards the door of his dreary oubliette[67], whereupon a shudder crawled down my spine at the sound

---

[66] *Risus Sardonicus:* Also 'Death's Head Grimace' – the unsettling contortion of the face in recently deceased.
[67] *Oubliette:* French – a 'forgotten place'.

of his voice;

"Goodbye, doctor."

Why had this parting troubled me so? What else was one expected to say at such a moment? No, it was all in the tone, that voice, such finality in his voice. Perhaps I was being fanciful; the weather here can have that effect. I must simply be overthinking the matter.

****

He was found dead this morning. May pity be with the unfortunate maid woman who discovered the corpse plummeted from his cell window. The night had passed without so much as a cry from his cell, leaving us puzzled as to the transpirations behind that damnable door. The mystery remaining will no doubt haunt my thoughts until the Lord takes me. *How was he able to climb from the window to initiate his fall?* The bars, interrogated extensively for their integrity, were found to be sturdy as an oak tree; with the gap betwixt them barely enough for a man's shoulder to pass through let alone his entire person. The shackle remained untampered. That iron which bound his ankle was locked, as it had been when it confined the foot, further compounding the mystery. Throughout the witching hours of the pre-dawn his door was guarded, and lest the warden fail spectacularly at his station, little explanation can be confirmed. Were he to *somehow* procure a key with which to escape his cell, how then does he come to fall from the very window within it? Impossible! Impossible!

****

Inveraray is to be closed. And whilst I had believed my poor brother Skallywag to find carnal salvation in the asylum at Hartwood, alas it would never be so. May God deliver that wretched man from the impossible evil that claimed him.

XXIV : From A London Newspaper, May 1889
Fire in downtown London claims three

Firefighters were called to a downtown residence near
Waterloo last night, following the outbreak of a massive
house fire. The call went out shortly after midnight after
nearby residents awoke to notice the blaze glowing in the
sky above the streets. By the time the crew had arrived the
house, known colloquially as Fairlie Estate, had become
completely engulfed in flames. Fairlie Estate is the opulent
home of Mister Ereven Fairlie, who was not home at the
time. The blaze is believed to have started during an
altercation between two men inside the house after a
curtain made contact with the lit fireplace. Police can
confirm the deaths of two women and one man who were
in the room when the fire began; the three believed to be
visitors to London. Meanwhile two men - both servants of
Fairlie - escaped unharmed; their names Mister Pinnacle
Tricks and Mister Atlas Egerton. The man killed is
believed to be Mister Walpole Wight, whose body remains
the only one of the three fatalities to be recovered.
According to Mister Tricks, Mister Wight appeared to have
fabricated his own death in a foiled plot to exact revenge
on some family grudge held with Mister Fairlie. Mister
Wight's twin daughters, Ague and Hemlocke, were
unfortunate victims in the botched plan, with firefighters
unable to recover the bodies. What began as a standard
house fire call has now escalated into a murder
investigation, with extraordinary claims that the perished
Mister Wight had intended to murder Mister Fairlie and

any associates. The investigation will continue in the coming days and the ruined home is being treated as a crime site. The owner of the home Mister Ereven Fairlie was not available to comment.

XXV : Resolutions

"Nevertheless, life and death are mysterious states, and we know little of the resources of either."

- J. Sheridan Le Fanu

When Vanesther Boucle awoke that particular morning she discovered inadvertently that Ereven Fairlie had kept his promise; he was gone. The window was open, the wind sent her transparent curtains fluttering and from beneath the weight of her coffee cup a note waved its corner.

Somehow I will make it right.

His parting words promised so much that they could never deliver. A strange sadness descended on her; although the spring sun shone cheerfully through her window, and the morning breeze spoke of a change for the better, she remained shaken by the recent events. Vanesther gazed out onto the street below, on the buildings beyond the Seine; it was a city that Brishen, her husband, would never know. The city known from her youth had changed, and she and her only ever love were no longer part of it. Time was invariably cruel to some. Like a starved wolf she drew on the first cigarette of the day and wonder whether she was better off knowing what she now knew. The question of Brishen's ultimate fate still loomed; even Faron, who had apparently been the last to see him, could not vouch for it.

As to whether she was better for having Faron return to her life, she would receive the answer weeks later in the form of another letter. Vanesther recognised the script, and its presence confirmed that the enigmatic man had not been an apparition.

It won't bring him back, but I hope it helps.

Were Walpole Wight alive to see his error, his rage would have increased all the more. For the will and testament concerning his 'fake' death stood as the most recent document regarding the distribution of his riches, and as such Fairlie had been left the sole benefactor upon his death in the London fire.

Ereven Fairlie, or Faron Silas, was never seen again. Having heard that his suspicions were correct and that his house had been destroyed he at last found the opportunity to properly express his remorse. In a stunning act of humility (an act so foreign to his life hitherto) he relinquished the vast fortune afforded to him through Walpole Wight to the woman who had given him the final chance he had begged for. Realising then that he'd far too many sins to atone for he slipped away from the life he had fabricated, and whether he found peace with himself or found others to call friends would remain unknown.

Atlas Egerton, having survived a brush with death, at long last cast off the shackles he had clasped himself into. With his master gone and the residence where he had lived and worked for decades destroyed, he took his first brave step into seizing the life he had remaining. Yes, his wife had passed, and maybe he didn't have many years left himself, but it was no reason to live in melancholy. His long unfinished poem – *'Gull and Leviathan'* - was at last completed, but it had taken the burning and destruction of his room (and any notes it contained) to bring it to a conclusion. Freed from the years of scribbles he'd scribed he rewrote the entire poem from memory, and when he'd punctuated the final line he closed his new poetry book and concluded that he may not open it again for some time. Spending so long on one idea had left him emotionally spent. In a casual converse with Pinnacle Tricks he shared his work, and was surprised to see the young man's face light up with an idea. Atlas' poem, set in a frigid locale, led Tricks to suggest he take up anchor with Cedrus and his crew, who were due to return to Reykjavik that very week. Despite his initial hesitation, the matter was settled, and Atlas Egerton was able to reverse decades of fret and torment in one drastic move.

And what of Pinnacle Tricks? Such answers were found in the pages of his final journal entry.

XXVI : The Final Journal of Pinnacle Tricks

"All this he saw, for one moment breathless and intense, vivid on the morning sky; and still, as he looked, he lived; and still, as he lived, he wondered."

-    Kenneth Grahame

I realise that quite some time has passed since my last entry; suffice to say I have needed nothing but time to sort through the experiences I've tackled in the last few months. Lord be praised for the comforts of home; I've at long last returned. To say I was overjoyed to see my wife would be quite the understatement, and given the way my strange tale ended, those feelings of joy were only increased, coupled also with an overwhelming thankfulness for life itself.

After the initial shock of that confrontation, all the puzzle pieces fell into line. Walpole Wight had never died. This enigmatic spectre had harboured some untold resentment towards Mr. Fairlie, and his will, the leaving of an estate to my superior - all of it a ploy to lure Fairlie into his trap. It is clear to me now, why Fairlie sent me to investigate the matter - and allow me to say in the privacy of this journal: he is a monster who I'll struggle to forgive as long as I walk this earth. He must have sensed the trap, yet the temptation of a fortune enticed him enough to use me as a shield. I had been expendable to him, and whatever the outcome, Fairlie would escape scot free. The only thing at risk was my life - the audacity! My blood boils at the thought! I'd ruined Wight's plans to murder Fairlie but my mere presence; he had intended to carry out his crime in the isolation of his own village, and when it had been me who turned up instead, he had had to think on his feet. His resulting plan was rushed, flawed, ill-thought out - yet I shiver to think that it came so close to completion.

Here I was concerned with hauntings and supernatural activity - curse my ignorance! Curse my childish anxiety! With the knowledge that Walpole Wight was alive, the unusual occurrences of my journey were all at once explainable. The 'ghosts' I had seen in the village, the forest, on the boat; the 'voice' I had heard at Wight Estate - all of it just the charade of a manic old man with a grudge outweighing his common sense. Yet still he fooled me long enough! Hemlocke's clandestine creeping about Cedrus' ship - Wight was there the whole time, following us back to London. She'd been nourishing the stowaway with her own rations, explaining the loss of appetite she had trumpeted.

Ague and Hemlocke - The Dryads, as Ague so lovingly titled them; I am still haunted by their deaths. Yet I remain conflicted by polarising feelings towards them. How much of their father's plot was known to them? It seems likely that they were in on the entire farce, Hemlocke in particular (a few question marks linger over Ague's ability to be so cunning). Should I mourn the death of friends who turned foe so swiftly? At times I feel partly responsible for their deaths, and at other times it would seem that they got what they deserved. Mayhaps that particular opinion should be left to the reader.

Then there was Wight's so-called fortune - I refuse to trouble myself with the thought. Whether there was in fact an inheritance to be claimed or not I know I will never see any money from this; better to forget it completely. Given the dilapidated state of Wight's old castle I would say that there is little to be claimed anyway. For whom, other than one as inhumane as Wight, could tolerate such a miserable existence in the North latitudes? Certainly not I. Fairlie has disappeared, his next of kin perished; I was just a pawn on his chessboard. I had thought myself the main protagonist of this story but instead was relegated to the background, just another puppet in some larger plot of which I knew nothing about and invariably still know very little. The more I think about it, the bitterness increases tenfold, and I am less satisfied with the conclusion. The termination of my contract with Mr. Fairlie - that too is a hollow victory, for I note again that the miserable old miser has disappeared. I've no doubt he caught wind of Wight's plot and is in hiding somewhere, while I obliviously led a wolf to the sheep. While I write this I feel that he probably did get his hands on the inheritance left for him and has run off for good. Mr. Egerton tells me that he has done it many times before. Again though, I am choosing not to trouble myself with the thought; my own suspicious nonsense has gotten me into strife before and I would like to think I am a little wiser now. Clearly I've a lot to learn of my craft, for it is clear to me now that not everything concludes the way one might have thought it would.

What I am left to ponder though is the extraordinary lengths people will go to for love. Hemlocke and Ague were willing to participate in their father's outrageous plans right to the very end, while conversely Wight and Fairlie demonstrated their extreme hatred to each other by risking the lives of others. I look at Viy and how he too had longed to return to his wife - and he had barely left her at home for any time at all! Cedrus and his adoration for his grandson, even the butler Atlas, whose melancholia has followed him ever since his wife's unfortunate passing. Love, honestly, floors me. For what else does one drop all pretence of self for the sake of another held dear to them? What else carries us through the darker days, swells our hearts at the very sight of a friend we might not have visited for a while? What brings us into line after a quarrel and sends us rushing to apologise, even if we are not at fault and merely wish to set things right? What brings tears to nostalgic memories, and anticipation to unknown futures - what else but love?

Of my own future I am uncertain, but I refuse to be fearful. There is little point in doubting my ability to sort matters out cleanly. After the journey I've partaken, I feel that little else will be quite as challenging. There is a great freedom in letting go of past misdemeanours, be they your own or a foe's, and I feel that whatever the travesty led to the feud between Wight and Fairlie, it irrevocably controlled their miserable lives. I do not plan to follow that same path of bitterness, for though life can have its unspeakable tragedies, there is simply too much joy out there for those who'd seek it.

ABOUT THE AUTHOR

Patrick Stephen Clinen (b.1988) lives in New South Wales, Australia. *The Will of the Wisp* is his second novel. His first novel, *Tenebrae Manor*, is a gothic fiction work published in 2014. His second work is *A Boy Named Art*, an illustrated children's poem. Both are available to purchase online. More poems, stories and other works by P.S.Clinen can be found at *www.psclinen.com*